Books by Robert Kimmel Smith

Sadie Shapiro

Matchmaker

Robert Kimmel Smith

Shelbyville–Shelby County Public Library

SIMON AND SCHUSTER
NEW YORK

Published by Simon and Schuster
A Division of Gulf & Western Corporation
Simon & Schuster Building
Rockefeller Center
1230 Avenue of the Americas
New York, New York 10020

Designed by Eve Kirch
Manufactured in the United States of America

1   2   3   4   5   6   7   8   9   10

Library of Congress Cataloging in Publication Data

Smith, Robert Kimmel, date.
    Sadie Shapiro, matchmaker.
        I. Title.
PZ4.S65823Sacg   [PS3569.M53795]   813'.5'4   79-20784
ISBN 0-671-24014-5

For Joan, with love

One

Somewhere on the avenue there had to be a taxi.

Sam Beck, his natty tan trench coat buckled tight to protect against the late spring breeze, stood at the curb in front of the Montana apartment house, a rather pallid imitation of the more famous Dakota two blocks farther south. Across the street, in Central Park, the huge Norway maple tree he and Sadie looked down on from their ninth-floor apartment was just coming into leaf. Spring in New York. Yesterday there had been hail and thunderstorms. In Poughkeepsie, three inches of snow had fallen. "Serves them right," Sam had told Sadie last evening as they watched the Eyewitness News Team throwing snowballs; "you want to live in Poughkeepsie, that's what you get."

"Taxi!" Down the street, a slow-moving Checker cab spotted Sam's upraised arm, cut across two lanes of traffic, and screeched to a halt at the curb. As Sam started forward, a woman brushed past him, yanked open the cab's door and leaped inside. "I'm awfully late—got to get downtown—very important—I'm sure you don't mind—thank you!" she threw at Sam in one unbroken sentence. She was middle-aged, with blond-streaked dark hair, and her eyes looked as if they hadn't been slept in for a week.

"Slow down," Sam said, "you'll live longer." He managed a grin. She was a pretty lady.

"Have a nice day," the woman said. "Whatever that means."

The cab pulled away and joined the traffic heading toward midtown. New York, New York, Sam thought, where your pulse rate's up and your battery runs down. Still, he loved this city. You knew you were alive here— in fact, no one would let you forget it—and if you could survive in New York City you could make it anywhere.

"Taxi!" A Yellow Cab pulled to the curb and Sam got in. "I want to go to Brooklyn. Court Street." Sam sat back in the seat.

The driver turned around and opened the plastic partition. He was a young Oriental, wearing thick-lensed horn-rimmed glasses. "Brooklyn? Where is Brooklyn?"

"You go down to lower Manhattan and turn left," Sam said, "you can't miss it."

The driver brightened. "Oh, over bridge, right?"

"Over bridge, left," Sam said. "Don't worry, I know the way."

Sam directed the driver through the park, across the East Side, and onto the FDR Drive. With only the Brooklyn Bridge ahead to navigate, he relaxed. His hand kept reaching to his breast pocket, feeling the five cigars there, but he resisted taking one out and lighting up. "You've got to cut down," Dr. Feingold had told him only last week when he went for his semi-annual check-up. "Twenty cigars a day is too much for a man your age."

"It's too much for a man *your* age, too," Sam had replied. Still, he would try to smoke fewer cigars. From now on, only nineteen a day.

He finally took out an Upmann Special and lit up. After all, how could he visit Brooklyn, his native heath, without making something special of it? He'd been born there, seventy-eight years ago on a freezing cold winter's day. Just recently, a young magazine writer interviewing Sadie had revealed that she too had been born in Brooklyn. "Which hospital were you born in?" she'd asked Sam. It had made him laugh. *Hospital?* He'd been born in his mother and father's bed, the same place he'd been conceived, in a cold-water flat on Gerry Street in Williamsburg. And there hadn't been any doctors around either. Just Mrs. Schaeffer, the local midwife, and Sam's Aunt Bessie, who knew about such things, having had seven children of her own. And the next day Sam's mother had been up and working again, sitting at the kitchen table sewing collars on housedresses. She got five cents a collar in those days, and the family needed every penny because Papa was selling fruit and vegetables from a wagon he drove through the streets, and at the end of the day he had to feed the horse.

Sam took a long pull on his cigar as the taxi sped across the Brooklyn Bridge. The day was sunny and the East River sparkled below, belying the fact that only the hardiest fish could survive its polluted waters. Sam wished that Sadie had come with him today. After visiting Levine, the lawyer, he would have taken her down to Coney Island for some sunning on the boardwalk, maybe a frozen custard. But Sadie was busy. (When wasn't she busy?) God bless her, she was a dynamo. This morning she was up in Central Park taping some commercials for

Channel 13, the local Public Broadcasting television station. The commercials were meant to promote a new PBS program, "Fitness and Health," on which Sadie had agreed to appear from time to time.

My wife the television star, Sam thought to himself. Sadie Shapiro had come a long way since the publication of her first knitting book had put her in the public eye. By now she was a regular guest on all the TV talk shows, had toured the country again on the publication of her second knitting book, and her efforts as a jogger had been featured in all the major magazines and television's "Wide World of Sports." Sadie was warm, Sadie was real, and people of all ages took to her, respecting her honesty and grandmotherly wisdom. For a woman who jogged a mile in an hour and ten minutes, she'd been moving very fast.

Sam took the lawyer's card from his pocket. Joseph S. Levine, Attorney at Law, 16 Court Street.

Levine had sounded very young on the telephone. "It's a bequest, Mr. Beck, that I'm handling very unofficially. An aunt of mine, a Mrs. Sarah Barish, passed away last week and I'm settling her affairs. She left something for Sadie Shapiro—your Sadie Shapiro—and I'd like to give it to you. Apparently my Aunt Sarah and your wife were good friends many years ago, when they were both young married women and next-door neighbors."

"That had to be fifty years ago," Sam said.

"I guess . . ."

"She left Sadie something in her will?"

Levine laughed. "Nothing as official as that. It's just a little package, and not very valuable. But why don't you come by and pick it up?"

At Sam's direction, the cab driver parked in front of 16 Court Street. The driver pulled the partition back and smiled as Sam paid him.

"And now you know where Brooklyn is," said Sam. "How long have you been driving a taxi?"

"Two day only."

"It figures."

"In America, two weeks only," the driver said proudly. "Uncle bring me and get me job."

"That's the way it worked in my family too, a long time ago. Did you come from the real China, or fake China?"

"No, no." The driver shook his head. "From Paris. Study there, in school, also work in restaurant." He handed Sam his change and then held onto his hand. "Someday I have restaurant in New York. You come eat there."

"Absolutely," Sam said, "and when you're ready, come to my neighborhood. We could use a new Chinese restaurant up there."

The young driver looked offended. "Not Chinese restaurant—*French* restaurant."

Joseph Levine was a well-built, good-looking young man with a head of thick, wavy black hair. He came out of an inner office when his secretary announced Sam and led him to a small conference room that overlooked lower New York Bay. Sam could see Governor's Island close at hand and in the distance, the Statue of Liberty. "I appreciate your coming to Brooklyn," Levine said. "I'm so busy I can't even get out for lunch. I've been writing briefs since seven o'clock this morning."

"And I've been wearing them since nine," Sam said.

Levine gave Sam a wary smile, as if something had passed by he hadn't quite caught. "Sit down," he said, "this won't take long." He took a bulky manila envelope off a bookshelf, then seated himself across the conference table from Sam. "Before I give you this, I have some

13

explaining to do. Does Sadie know anything about my Aunt Sarah's later life?"

"Nothing," Sam shrugged. "They hadn't seen or heard from each other in so many years . . ."

"Of course," Levine nodded. "For the past ten years, my Aunt Sarah was a matchmaker."

"No kidding." Sam grinned. "I didn't realize matchmakers still existed."

"Oh yes, they do. Of course, my Aunt Sarah didn't make a business of it. She did it for the *mitzvah*, the joy of doing a good deed. She started with a neighbor, who asked Sarah to be on the lookout for a nice young boy who might be right for her daughter. Sarah didn't have much else to do—her son and daughter-in-law had moved away, she had been widowed for several years—and the long and short of it was that Sarah found a fellow, matched him with the neighbor's daughter, the two of them clicked and got married."

"And that started her off."

"Exactly," Levine said. "After she made her first match, word got around and people started coming to her. In ten years she matched forty couples, which they tell me is a very good average."

Sam lit a cigar and put the dead match in the ashtray. "And where does Sadie come into this?"

"I'm getting there," Levine said.

The young attorney rubbed his chin with the back of a hand. "Sarah knew she was dying about six months ago. And she was very worried—not so much for herself, but for the people she was trying to match up. She passed most of them on to other matchmakers, keeping tabs to see how they were faring, but a few she kept for herself. These were her 'special-specials,' people other matchmakers wouldn't take. Just before she died, Sarah gave me this package. 'This is for Sadie Shapiro,' she said, 'and

14

make sure it gets into her hands.'" Levine pushed the bulky envelope across the table.

Sam unfastened the clasp and opened the envelope. From inside he withdrew a small tin box, brightly colored, that used to contain Swee-Touch-Nee tea. Inside the box, Sam saw three index cards with notations written in a small spidery hand. "Her special-specials," he said.

Levine nodded. "There's also a note."

Sam took a piece of pink notepaper from the tea box. Unfolding it, he began to read:

Dear Sadie:
Here is a hello that is also a goodbye. From your friend Sarah Barish who lived next door to you on Carroll Street for so many years.

By now you already know about my match-making and why I can't continue any more. Sadie —I had so much joy from this. It's like doing God's work.

Somehow, I always thought that when I matched up my last person, and took the name out of my tea box, that then I could find my final rest.

But I was wrong, Sadie, and the end is coming sooner than I thought. I still got three names left in my matchmaking box—three people I couldn't match up—and I turn to you to finish my work.

Please, Sadie, I beg of you, take care of them. Find them husbands and wives to make them happy. I know you'll do this thing, because I know how you always said a "Shapiro never quits."

So, Sadie, do this one last thing for me, who never forgot you, and, may it bring you joy like it brought me.

With love, your friend,
Sarah

Sam slowly refolded the letter and put it into the tea box.

"Sarah was a sweet lady," Levine said.

"I can see that." In the ashtray, his cigar had gone cold. There was a long silence as Sam and the young attorney sat quietly. Then Sam closed the tea box and put it back into the manila envelope.

"So," Levine said, getting up, "I kept my word to Sarah. You'll take the box to Sadie?"

Sam nodded. "She'll have it this evening."

"Good." Sam picked up the envelope and Levine walked with him through the outer office and to the hallway door. He shook Sam's hand, then drew him closer. "Look," he said in a very low voice, "you understand that Sadie doesn't have to do this. I mean . . . there's nothing legally binding here."

"I know."

"Sadie should do what she wants," Levine said. "There's really no obligation."

Sam's smile was thin and fleeting. "Counselor," he said, "I think you still have a few things to learn about obligation."

Two

She came jogging along the macadam path, heading for the vast meadow in Central Park. A slim, slightly built woman of undetermined age, moving in a rhythm peculiar to herself, bouncing along at a crisp one mile per hour, feet lifting high, taking short choppy steps, giving the overall effect of a small child riding a pogo stick. She was wearing a bright pink hand-knitted sweat suit of her own design. On her head, a matching tam o'shanter. On her feet, a pair of well-worn Puma joggers. On her back, concealed beneath her sweat suit, a battery-pack to power the wireless microphone clipped neatly to her collar.

Inside the mobile PBS television tape truck parked some distance away, five people sat before the control board, watching Sadie Shapiro's jogging figure on half a dozen color TV monitors. "Looking good," said the director, Fred Dubin. "Stay with her, Camera Two . . . good . . ."

A wheezing sound, something like air being forced from a punctured balloon, came through the speaker system in the truck. "What's that?" Dubin asked. "Sound, do you hear it?"

The sound engineer shrugged. "It must be her. The old lady."

"Why is she doing that?" Dubin demanded. "This is supposed to be silent."

"It's just her breathing," said the young woman with the Modigliani nose; "not to worry. We'll edit it out later." Maxine Morris looked over at Dubin, whose low boiling point was well-known in the industry. As producer of the upcoming PBS series "Fitness and Health," Maxine was responsible for taping this commercial to promote the show, as well as several others. Fred Dubin had not been her first choice as director, nor her tenth, for that matter. He was a difficult man to work with, although a brilliant director, and she meant to ride herd on his temper before it got out of hand.

"Amateur night," Dubin growled. "Ready, Camera Three . . ."

Over the loudspeaker in the truck, there came a different sound.

"Train the body, don't strain the body," Sadie Shapiro was saying, "and jog straight ahead across the horse path and onto the grass . . ."

"Oh, God!" Dubin muttered.

"Don't worry about it," Maxine said quickly.

". . . and when I jog up to the little piece of green tape I stop and say what they told me, who knows if I'll remember, but I'll do my best and remember to smile, like they said I should, and then I jog away and across the meadow . . ."

"She's nuts!" Dubin exploded.

"It's okay, Freddie," Maxine said, "we'll be covering this part with music anyway."

". . . Feet, you're doing splendid, keep it up," said Sadie.

"We'll be here for sixteen takes, wanna bet?" Dubin said.

"We've got all morning, Freddie, calm down," Maxine said. Gold flecks danced in her green eyes as her own temper began to rise.

". . . Heart, you're doing splendid down there," Sadie was saying. "Lungs—just keep breathing." But now, in addition to Sadie's voice, there was another sound coming over the speaker.

"Sound!" Dubin snapped, "what's that?"

The engineer cocked his head as he listened closely. "Sounds like . . . *hoofbeats?*"

"Oh, no!" Maxine exclaimed, "the horse path!"

The wide shot on the middle TV monitor showed what was happening. There was Sadie Shapiro, jogging straight for the camera, concentrating for all she was worth, about to cross the bridle path. And there, emerging from a copse of trees, was a snow-white horse and rider coming at a rapid canter on a collision course. Unless Sadie or the horse veered away, they were destined to meet.

"Stop tape!" Dubin shouted.

"Stop Sadie!" Maxine shouted. "Camera Three—*stop her!*"

Up on the TV screen the action was being played out. Like the Titanic and that infamous berg, Sadie and the snow-white horse ran toward each other in living color. Sadie was on the cinder path now, the horse a stride away. With a thump that was audible in the truck, they met, and Sadie was suddenly and violently thrown to the ground.

Maxine ripped off her headset and was out of the truck and running. Behind her, Fred Dubin and the sound man gave chase. Sadie was still down, not moving, and a pair of cameramen were at her side. The horse and rider were nowhere to be seen.

Breathless, Maxine reached the inert form of Sadie Shapiro and knelt beside her.

Sadie's eyelids fluttered and she groaned. She opened her eyes, closed them, then opened them again. "Hello," she said. "Where am I?"

"Take it easy," Maxine said. She clutched Sadie's hand and for want of something better to do, began rubbing it.

"What hit me?" Sadie said.

"A horse."

"A what?"

"Never mind that," Maxine said. "How are you?"

"A horse," Sadie said. "Did you get his license plate number?"

"He ran away," Maxine said.

"Hit by a hit-and-run horse," Sadie said. "Every day, a new adventure."

"How do you feel?" Fred Dubin asked.

"I don't know," Sadie said. "All the pieces are here, but right now they don't feel like they belong to the same person, if you get my drift. Maybe I should sit up."

"Don't you move," Maxine commanded.

Sadie grasped Maxine's hand and sat up, then began patting herself all over. "Two arms, two legs, one body and one head. So far, so good."

"Sadie," Maxine said, "you really shouldn't move yet. Something might be broken."

"If you only knew how many parts are already broken from years ago," Sadie said with a grin. Slowly she got to her feet. "There you are, fat as a fiddler and good as new."

Suddenly she swayed and grasped her middle, on her face a grimace of pain.

Maxine took hold of her. "Sadie!"

"It's only my gall bladder, or maybe my liver," Sadie said. "A woman my age, you eat a piece of fried fish, you take your life in your mouth."

"Are you all right?"

"Fine, perfect," Sadie said. "In a hundred years I'll feel better, if not sooner."

From out of the trees came the sound of hoofbeats, followed by a white horse and rider. The horse looked nervous, cantering sideways as the rider brought him near. "Easy, Silver, easy boy," the rider called out. He was a young, good-looking man, wearing faded jeans and scuffed boots. He brought the horse near and dismounted. "I'm sorry," he began to say, but Maxine interrupted.

"Idiot! Are you insane?"

"I'm sorry . . . she came running right into us . . . I didn't see her."

Maxine's eyes flashed. "They ought to take your horse away, riding like that. You could have killed her."

"I said I'm sorry," the young man replied. "And I didn't mean to run off that way, but Silver bolted and it took some time to bring him in check."

"Is that the horse's name," Sadie asked, "Silver?"

"And he's The Lone Ranger, obviously," Maxine said.

"I'm Michael Newman, actually," the young man said, smiling, "but you can call me 'Lone.' "

Maxine stared hard at Newman. "That's not funny, and this is no time for jokes."

"You're perfectly right," Newman said pleasantly. He turned to Sadie. "Let me apologize again. It was very stupid of me not to see you."

"Apology accepted," Sadie said, and meant it. There

was something very winning about Michael Newman, his smile perhaps, or the honest look in his deep brown eyes. Sadie warmed to him instantly.

"May I examine you?" he asked Sadie, and without waiting for an answer began feeling her arms and legs.

"Just a second here," Sadie protested.

"I'm a doctor," Newman said, "it's all right." He began unzipping her sweat suit jacket.

"What kind of doctor?"

"Surgeon," Newman said, "a plastic surgeon." He pushed Sadie's jacket aside and bared her left shoulder.

"How do we know you're really a doctor?" Maxine said.

"You don't," Newman said matter of factly. He looked closely at Sadie's shoulder, then manipulated her arm. "Does that hurt?" he asked.

"No."

"Good. You'll have a nasty bruise there, but I don't think any bones are broken. If you'd like to come to my office, I'll take some x-rays."

"No," Sadie said. "I'm fine. As well as anybody hit by a horse. Just for a minute there I was a little *nonpulsed,* that's all."

Newman smiled at Sadie. "I think you'll be fine, too."

"No thanks to you," Maxine said.

Michael Newman had heard enough biting comments from the young woman at his side. He turned to her, intending to say something nasty, but when he looked at her his expression softened at once. He looked into her deep-set green eyes, saw her auburn hair that had copper highlights in the sun, her generous lips and firm upthrust chin, and something stirred inside him. What a nose she had, so long and straight and oddly attractive. He wanted to reach out and stroke it, or better yet, plant a gentle kiss on it. For noses were a good part of the surgery Newman performed. He'd seen hooked ones and flat ones, bulbous ones and bent ones, and always the young women involved wanted them cut and reshaped into a snub, a pug, a tiny peninsula. This girl had a nose that was a nose. And she wore it like a queen. "Don't ever change that nose," said Michael Newman.

Maxine stared, not sure she had heard correctly.

"It's beautiful," he said, "and so are you. What's your name?"

Sadie made introductions all around, but Newman couldn't take his eyes away from Maxine's face. "Can I buy you a cup of coffee?" he asked.

"No."

"Can I see you sometime? Date you, I mean?"

Maxine shook her head.

"How do I get in touch with you?"

"You don't," Maxine said. "Now run along."

"I'll be in touch," Michael Newman said. He shook Sadie's hand, apologized once more, and mounted Silver.

"It was very nice running into you," Sadie said.

"Same here," said Michael Newman.

With a grin for Maxine, the young surgeon rode away on his horse as Dubin and Sadie stood looking.

"What a nice young man," Sadie said. "And so handsome."

"He's an idiot," Maxine said.

"Sha-sha," Sadie shushed, "that's no way to talk about the man you're going to marry."

Three

She had bathed and had dinner and now, dressed in her favorite old flannel nightgown with the tea stain on the hem, she was rereading the letter for the third time. Sarah Barish, the Matchmaker . . . a voice from the past she would hear no more. How many years ago had they been close friends? Too many.

"So I told this Levine fella that I would give you the package," Sam was saying, "and that knowing you, you would do what Sarah asked."

"Of course," Sadie nodded, sighing. "Sarah was a friend only your best friends should have. A dear, sweet woman, and when we lived next door to each other we were like sisters."

Sam took a long pull on his Upmann Special. "So, on top of everything else that you're doing, it looks like you're in the matchmaking business."

"For a friend you've got to do," Sadie said, "especially when your friend is dead and you're not." She put the letter down on the lamp table. "What a lively person Sarah was, busy as a hen with one chicken, always running, always doing. And happy . . . all the time. Even though when I knew her it was supposed to be the Depression, if you remember that."

"Who can forget? It was in all the newspapers and everything."

"Her husband was in ladies' handbags and from one day to the next Sarah never knew if she was rich or poor. But when Sarah had money, we all had money." Sadie smiled for a moment. "One time Sarah took a whole bunch of us girls to a fancy restaurant. And during the meal the waiter put down in front of us these finger bowls. Now you have to remember that we were all poor girls, and not one of us had ever seen anything as fancy-shmancy as a finger bowl before. So I looked at Sarah, and she looked at me, and nobody knew what to do until Sarah said, 'salad dressing!' "

"Oh, no."

"Oh, yes. And we all poured those finger bowls right over our salad," Sadie said, with a laugh. "That was Sarah to a tee, let her rest in peace." Sighing, Sadie looked at the tin tea box on the table. "Matchmaking," she shrugged, "who knows from matchmaking?"

Sam couldn't believe his ears. "You do."

"Me?"

"Do you have to teach a duck to swim? You're a natural, my love. Matchmaking is your middle name."

"Oh, that reminds me," said Sadie, "I forgot to tell you what happened today in the park when the horse knocked me down."

Sam looked at Sadie. "Horse?"

"The nicest young man, Michael Newman, a doctor, and I could just see by the look on his face what he was thinking about our own Maxine, from the TV show."

"A horse knocked you down?"

"And Maxine, you know her temper by now, she got up on her high horse and off on the wrong foot with him right away. A doctor, mind you!"

"Whoa there!" Sam said, holding up a hand. When Sadie got started on a tale, sometimes the words could flow like Niagara. "You got hit by a horse today?"

"Oh, that," Sadie shrugged. "It was a little accident, a piffle, a nothing. I just ran into a horse, or he ran into me, and he almost killed me, that's all. Not worth talking about. But for Maxine I think it's the beginning of a beautiful tomorrow, if you take my meaning and if she were smart she would too. How many girls have a future husband come riding up on a big white horse?"

"Very few," Sam said, "except in cowboy pictures."

"Exactly."

"But I've got news for you," Sam said. "I don't think Maxine Morris is crazy to find a husband. She's got her career and all, and I think she's happy the way she is."

"Wrong," Sadie said. "In their heart of hearts, every girl wants a husband, if they'll only admit it, and Maxine is no exception. And I could see from the look on his face that Michael Newman is already in love with her."

"So fast you could tell?"

"Do you have to step outside and get wet to know it's raining? Of course, I could tell."

"Then Maxine had better watch out." Sam took hold of the old tin tea box with the three cards inside and handed it to Sadie. "All right, matchmaker," he said, "do your stuff."

Sadie took the three index cards out of the tea box and they began looking at them together.

"The widow Mandelbaum," Sam said. "I know her building on Park Avenue. If she lives there, she must be rich."

```
Mandelbaum, Doris   (widow)  Age: 50+
701 Park Ave  Apt 12-A   PL-9- 8667
     Good-looking woman, probably rich. Stunning Apt.
wants man not too much older than self. Should
be bright, cultured—does not have to be handsome—
but must have money. (Very Important)
Dates: 3/26-No  4/11-No  5/3-No  5/8-No  5/23-No
7/14-No   9/15- No  9/30-No  10/3-No  11/17-No
12/4- No   1/6-No
```

"And if Sarah wrote down she's good-looking, then she's probably gorgeous."

Sam nodded. "A rich, good-looking, Park Avenue widow. I don't think you'll have any trouble finding someone for her."

Sadie's bony finger ticked the bottom half of the card. "Twelve men she already said 'no' to, Sam. That's trouble right there."

Sadie turned to the next card.

```
WALD, Harry  (widower)   Age 56
219 Joralemon St. - Apt 10-C   BU-4-3571
Brooklyn

  clean, plain-looking man, poor dresser. Wants
warm, quiet woman -good cook. Homebody essential.
Dates: 6/11 - No    8/14 -No    9/11-No  9/15-No
   10/3 - Liked her- she didn't like him  12/3-No
   2/25 - No
```

"Joralemon Street is over in Brooklyn Heights, not a bad neighborhood," Sam said. "What do you think Sarah meant when she wrote here 'plain-looking'?"

"Not Cary Grant."

"Ahah. And 'poor dresser'? What's that mean?"

"I think Sarah, knowing how kind she was, didn't want to write something worse."

Sam smiled thinly. "So Mister Harry Wald is probably some kind of poor shnook, not your ideal matchmaker material. Oh well, at least I see here on the card he met one woman he liked. That's a hopeful sign."

"I also see on the card that the woman he liked didn't like him. And six others this Mister Wald didn't like, either."

"So Harry Wald is problem number two."

Sadie nodded, and turned over the next index card.

```
Fogelman, Brenda              Age-24
41 Mercer Street              No phone
                             Call Doll Factory
Does not want to get married.
Try — as favor for cousin Leah.
Saw her for 10 minutes and threw me out.
Dates: 6/27 - Threaten could not get to see her -No
       11/15 - Had argument - No
       2/3 — Thought Brenda looked like man - NO
```

After reading Brenda Fogelman's card, Sadie uttered a quiet sigh. How did Sarah take on as a matchmaking client a young girl who plainly must have told her she did not want to get married? She thought back to the past for a moment, then remembered. "I once met Sarah's Cousin Leah," she said.

"And?"

"The whole family was crazy, that's what I remember."

Sam groaned. "It says here that Sarah saw this Fogelman girl and got thrown out for her pains. Also, she sent her three fellas and one of them argued with her, another couldn't get to see her, and the third one thought she looked like a man."

"That sounds like Leah's family."

"Oh, boy!" Sam shook his head. "She lives down in SoHo, probably in a cage. And naturally, no telephone. What's this note here: 'Call doll factory'?"

Sadie shrugged. "So these are Sarah's special-specials . . ."

"A rich widow who's rejected twelve men, a poor shnook from Brooklyn, and a young girl who doesn't want to get married." Chuckling at the impossibility of such a collection, he got Sadie to smile. "So, matchmaker, what are we going to do?"

"First," Sadie said, "first, we'll have a cup of tea."

Two hours later they were still talking.

"I'm beginning to see that being a real matchmaker, instead of just a buttinsky like me, is not so easy," Sadie was saying. "I mean, everybody else I matched up I already knew the two people involved. But what do I have here? Three cards and three names. People I don't know from a whole wall."

Sam had a yellow legal pad on his lap and he made a note. "Okay, number one, you've got to meet these three people. That's not so hard."

"It will take time, and time I haven't got, Sam. Not with doing these commercials, and then taping some programs, and thinking about my new knitting book."

Sam thought for a moment. "I got an idea. Instead of you running around finding Doris Mandelbaum, Harry Wald, and Brenda Fogelman, why don't you invite them all here?"

Sadie's face brightened. "Good idea. Let the mountain come to Moe Hammid. Terrific!" She stood up from her chair, stretched for a few seconds, then began to pace the room. "Wait a minute," she said. "I think I got another brainstorm. Why don't we have a party for them? Invite all three of them up here at one time so I can get to know them. Is that a good idea?"

"Sure."

"And how's this for better?" Sadie went on. "We *also* invite some nice eligible people for all three of them to meet!"

"Now you're talking," Sam said.

"So while we're all saying 'how do you do?' and all that, maybe lightning will strike and they'll meet somebody right away, they should be so lucky. Wouldn't that be a blessing?"

"It'd be a miracle."

"But still," Sadie said, "it's worth a try, right? If you don't chop meat, you don't have a hamburger."

"Or whatever."

"That's it," Sadie declared. "We have a matchmaking party right here and with a little luck, we'll find people for this Mrs. Mandelbaum, Harry Wald, and Brenda Fogelman, whoever they are, and my job will be over." A sudden dark cloud passed over Sadie's face and she sank into a chair. "Ay-yi-yi, I just realized what kind of problem we got. Where am I going to find a whole bunch of eligible people?"

Sam flicked an inch of ash into the marble ashtray. "You're right," he said, his forehead wrinkling as he thought about it. "Now I see how matchmakers operate.

You not only got to have index cards of people wanting to get married, you got to have real live people to match them up with."

"Exactly."

"I could print up handbills and go give them out in Times Square," Sam said. "That'd get people."

"Be serious," Sadie said. "I'm talking nice, eligible people who want to find a mate, not *nudniks.* Especially for this Mrs. Mandelbaum and Harry Wald, who are over fifty. The only eligible people I know that age are either married already or dead."

"Oh, boy," Sam sighed, "we got a problem."

"So start thinking," Sadie said. "Who and where to find people for matching." She looked at Sam and giggled. "Abe Farkas?"

Sam looked scornfully over his cigar. "Abe Farkas is almost seventy years old, Sadie. It's true he's a widower, and a fine man, but he's a little old for Mrs. Mandelbaum, don't you think?"

"He's alive and breathing," Sadie said. "Call him."

Before Sam could reply, the doorbell rang. He rose and walked through the little foyer to the door. It was Bryna Pernik, the young woman who lived in an apartment down the hall. In her hand she carried a plate with a slice of cake on it. "Again with the fruitcake?" Sam said.

"It's only the curse of my life," Bryna said. "Is Sadie in?"

Nodding, Sam followed the short Hungarian emigrée into the living room. Bryna Pernik had been three years old in 1956, when the short-lived revolution in Budapest had allowed several hundred thousand of her people to flee the country. For the past fifteen years she had lived in New York. She was a bright, hard-working young girl with a quicksilver smile, and Sadie liked her very much.

Bryna had set her heart on being an outstanding cook, and she operated a party catering business from her apartment.

"Another fruitcake?" Sadie asked Bryna.

"Try it," Bryna said. She handed the plate and a fork to Sadie, and watched while she tasted it. "Too dry, right?"

"Yes," said Sadie, "and it's missing something."

"I'll kill her," Bryna said, "I'll murder her."

"Don't kill and don't murder," Sadie said, "especially not your own grandmother."

"Can you tell me why she's keeping it a secret?" Bryna demanded. "My own grandmother makes a fruitcake like no other in the whole world. Fantastic! Delicious! You know how important that can be for me at Christmas time, that cake? It could make me a household word for catering! And will she give me her recipe? Not on your life. Why?"

"Grandmothers are grandmothers," Sadie shrugged.

"It's not the plans for an atomic bomb," Bryna said, "it's a fruitcake. And so is she."

Sam took Sadie's fork and tasted the cake. "Dry is right," he said. "I liked yesterday's better."

"You would," Bryna said, scowling, "that was lousy, too. What's this, the fifth fruitcake I brought in here this week?"

"And don't forget the three from last week," Sam said.

"They were awful," Bryna said. "I'm going out of my mind, baking fruitcakes, when my grandmother already has the recipe for the best one I ever tasted."

"Maybe you'll be lucky and invent a terrific fruitcake all on your own," Sadie said.

"And maybe I'll grow another body and be a Siamese twin," Bryna said. She raised her hand in a fist and shook it in the direction of her grandmother's apartment, across

Central Park on the East Side. "Back to the drawing board," she said, and without another word she took the cake plate and marched out of Sadie's apartment.

"Eight million stories in the naked city, and we get a Hungarian fruitcake," said Sam.

"Bryna's a lovely girl," Sadie said, "and I won't hear a bad word about her. Her grandmother . . . that's a different story."

"If we ever find people to come to your matchmaking party, Bryna can cater it," Sam said.

"Right," Sadie nodded. "So why don't you invite the first guest, Abe Farkas?"

"I'm telling you, Sadie, Abe is too old for that Mandelbaum lady, and his prostate is acting up again. Believe me, marriage is not on his mind."

"It's a start," Sadie said, "and I'll love to see him, anyway. And a good idea would be to tell him to bring a friend."

Sam picked up the telephone and dialed Abe Farkas. "Hello, kiddo, it's Sam," he said. "Listen, have I got a girl for you . . ."

Four

Harry Wald sat in the faded club chair with the greasy headrest, watching a freighter cross lower New York Bay. Otto, the seven-year-old tabby cat, sat on his lap, purring as Harry slowly stroked the back of his neck.

So, he thought, the old matchmaker is dead, which is why he hadn't heard from her in several weeks. And the woman he had just spoken with on the telephone, Sadie Shapiro . . . he knew her from somewhere. . . . Her voice sounded so familiar, lively and energetic. Wait a minute . . . the lady with the knitting books! He'd seen her on television. *That* Sadie Shapiro, of course . . .

"So what do you think, Otto?" he asked the cat. "Should we go to that party, or not? Do I need a wife?"

Could anyone ever take the place of his Emily? For twenty-seven years she had brightened his life. Emily with the quick smile, the dark brown hair that came to her shoulders, the gentle hands that stroked his neck even as he stroked the cat. To lose a woman like that, so young, still with years to live and laugh and be happy . . .

Living alone was not living. A man should have a wife, a soul must have a soul. The silence in this old apartment was deafening. To come home and not say a word to anyone from night till morning was not a natural way to live. And to sleep alone . . .

He would go to Sadie Shapiro's party—and maybe, *maybe*, there would be a woman there.

Doris Mandelbaum circled the date on the calendar that hung by the telephone in the kitchen. She was still smiling to herself over her conversation with Sadie Shapiro. Imagine, *the* Sadie Shapiro was going to search out a husband for Doris Mandelbaum!

One of the pastimes she had taken up in her widowhood was knitting. Which had led her to Sadie's first knitting book, and then her second, and then to a knitting demonstration at Bloomingdale's where she had met and talked with Sadie herself. That was no more than a year ago. It's funny how life is a circle, she thought, and sometimes you can meet yourself on the way around.

She thought for a moment of the old matchmaker, and of her passing. How many candidates had Sarah Barish sent, and how many had she cast away? Each one deficient in some way. No one measured up to her Jacob, may he rest in eternal peace.

Jacob . . . what a fine figure of a man he had been. So tall, so filled with life and energy, and how gentle with her. The feel of him beside her in the bed, the solid warmth of his body, those strong arms encircling her. His fine taste in music, in art, in the clothes he wore. The joy she felt strolling with Jacob on a Sunday afternoon, looking into the galleries on Madison Avenue, discussing the pictures in the museum, the pride she felt just listening to him.

No, there would not be another Jacob in her life, that

she knew. But she would not settle for a nobody, a nothing. To have a Jacob once in your life was already a miracle. There would be no second one. But somewhere, someone, if only to fill Jacob's shadow and give meaning to the rest of her life . . .

Thinking thus, she wandered through the apartment, ending at the clothes closet in the bedroom. The black wool sheath dress, of course. She would wear that to Sadie Shapiro's party. With just the Buccellati choker Jacob had bought for her in Florence. Or perhaps that gold-trimmed jade pin . . .

The cab drew up on an industrial street in lower Manhattan. "This is where Brenda Fogelman lives?" Sadie's eyes scanned the neighborhood. "It's all factories here, Sam."

"This is where she lives," Sam said. He finished paying the taxi driver and joined Sadie on the sidewalk. A man pushing a hand truck loaded with auto parts brushed by them. "Why, in this day and age, doesn't she have a telephone?" Sam said. "Making us *shlep* down to this Godforsaken place."

"From the look around here she's probably a poor girl," Sadie said. "Maybe that's why she has no phone."

"Nobody's that poor," Sam said. "Even when my family couldn't rub two nickels together, we had a telephone. Of course, it was in the candy store on the corner and they had to send a kid to call us on the phone . . ." Grumbling, Sam checked the address on the card and led Sadie to the door. There was a worn metal sign on the wall next to the door listing the occupants of the building. Ackerman Electrical, Bitsey Baby Dolls, Sobel Lampworks, Tauber Printing. No Brenda Fogelman. "I'll check," Sam said. He walked down the dark and dusty hall and stuck his head inside Ackerman Electrical. A clerk sat behind a counter, reading the *Daily News.* "Is there a Brenda Fogelman in this building?"

"Who?"

"Miss Brenda Fogelman."

The clerk shrugged. He turned toward the rear and shouted at the top of his voice: "Hey, Charlie! You know a Brenda Fogelman?"

After an instant a voice shouted back: "The weirdo on the top floor!"

"Thank you," Sam said to the clerk.

"She's the weirdo on the top floor," the clerk said. He went back to his newspaper and Sam went back to Sadie in the hallway. "She's on the top floor," he said.

"I heard. And she's also a weirdo."

Sam walked to the back of the hallway and then returned. "I got news for you," he said, "there's no elevator."

"Then we go up the stairs."

"Six flights?" Sam stared at Sadie. "I wouldn't climb six flights for the Pope."

"Popes don't get married," Sadie said. "Come."

The stairs and landings were as dimly lit and dirty as the rest of the building. On the second floor landing Sam paused to catch his breath. He inspected the small bulb on the wall burning inside its protective wire cage. "How do you like that?" he said. "I never knew they made a five-watt bulb."

On the fourth floor landing, Sam was puffing again, and by the fifth floor he was ready to quit. "I think my ears just closed," he gasped with a grin, then hurried to catch up with Sadie. Gaining the top floor, Sam held on to iron banister for support. Across the landing was a door, painted black, and on it a piece of wide masking tape where Brenda Fogelman had scrawled her name with a felt tip pen.

"I hope she's home," Sadie said.

"If not, I kill myself," Sam gasped. Twenty cigars a day and no exercise, he said to himself, dummy. Sadie the jogger looked as if she could climb another six flights and then dance a jig at the top.

Sadie knocked and a voice shouted come in. She opened the door to a vast open space, with grimy skylights flooding the room with sunlight. Far off, perhaps thirty feet away, a figure in coveralls and a black welding mask stood hunched over a piece of heavy metal, making sparks fly as the welding torch hissed and flamed.

"Excuse me, Mister," Sadie said, "I'm looking for Brenda Fogelman."

The figure stood straight, extinguished the torch, turned up the welding mask to reveal a dirty, though unmistakably feminine face. "That's me. What the hell do you want?"

Sadie regarded her with a feeling of disbelief. An oval face was revealed beneath the welding mask, with wide, heavy eyebrows and coal black eyes. If you disregarded the smudged cheeks, the tangle of wild, black hair peeking out from under the mask, and the total lack of lipstick and makeup, Brenda Fogelman had the makings of an attractive young lady.

"I said what do you want!" Brenda barked.

"You said worse than that," Sadie replied, "and you should watch your language because if you start talking like that others talk back to you the same way and then we got half the world cursing, if you get my drift, and I see that you do because of the look on your face."

Brenda blinked twice and looked at Sam. "Is she with you?"

"Forever, I hope," Sam said. His breath was starting to return.

"I'm Sadie Shapiro," said Sadie Shapiro, "and I came

to see you because the matchmaker, Sarah Barish, passed away, let her rest in peace, and she gave me your name to find a husband, and if you're willing, I'm willing, so why don't we get to know each other a little better."

"So that's it," Brenda said. She put down her welding torch, wiped her hands on a rag, and came walking over to Sadie. "Look—I told my Aunt Leah and I told Sarah Barish—leave me alone with the matchmaking. I'm not interested in finding a husband, not until I get my act together, and maybe not even then. I just want to be left alone in peace to do my work, okay?" She brushed her smudged cheek with the back of her hand, which spread the dirt as far back as her ear.

"Wouldn't dream of interrupting your work," Sadie said. She glanced at the jumble of metal parts littering the floor. "What is your work, anyway? It looks like you're making a car, or something."

"I'm a sculptor," Brenda said.

Sadie's smile was wide. "How do you like that, an artist! I'm always glad to meet an artist because I'm something in that line myself, what with designing my own knitting patterns and everything."

A look of recognition crossed Brenda's face. "Oh, you're *that* Sadie Shapiro! The woman with the knitting books. I've seen you on television." She thrust out her dirty hand and took Sadie's in a grip of steel. "Glad to meet you. You're a right-on woman."

"Right on *what*?" Sadie asked as, wincing, she took her hand back.

"Just right-on," Brenda said. "Hey, would you like to see my work? I'm going nonstop because I'm going to have a one-woman show at a gallery next month, but I'd be glad to show you everything."

"Why not?" Sadie said. The more she knew about

Brenda Fogelman, the easier it would be to find the right man for her, she thought. At the moment, that would be a man who liked a girl who looked like a man. Also, he'd have to not mind living in a field of rubble, because Brenda's place looked more like a junkyard than a home. Sadie shuddered as Brenda stepped over her mattress on the way to the far wall.

Brenda pointed at a structure of smooth metal that came as high as Sadie's chin. "I call this 'American Rustic,'" she said.

"Of course," Sadie nodded, "it's very rusted. Maybe if you used a Brillo pad, a little soap and water . . ."

"Sure," Brenda nodded, although she didn't know why. She led Sadie through her collection of pieces, pride in her voice as she explained the workmanship that had gone into each piece of sculpture. To Sadie, they all looked very much alike: twisted and jumbled pieces of dirty metal heaped together to form a pile. That they represented art in some form was beyond comprehension. But then, she had once seen a painting by a Jackson Pollack that people said was very important. To Sadie, it had looked like the old dropcloth the workmen had used when they painted her living room.

"Very nice," Sadie said, "and I wish you a lot of luck with it."

"Thanks," Brenda grinned. "So you see why I'm working so hard. I've got half a dozen pieces to finish before my show. That doesn't leave time for anything else."

"You could take one evening out," Sadie said. "I'm having this party and inviting a lot of people, and you never know—there could just be someone you'll meet there."

"I'll take a pass on that," Brenda said.

"You don't need a pass, you just walk in to my apartment."

"Not interested," Brenda said.

"Just like that?"

"Just like that," Brenda repeated. "Look, I'm not into men right now. My work is everything. Men just . . . I don't know, they get in the way."

"What are you talking?" Sadie said. "Men are terrific, especially the ones you marry. If it wasn't for my Reuben, let him rest, and my wonderful Sam, who knows where I'd be today."

"You've been lucky," Brenda said. "Marriage is for the birds."

"And for the bees, and for all the animals, too, if you'll remember in the Bible how they got on the Ark two by two, not one by one. Not another word against marriage, Brenda please, because without marriage you wouldn't be here and neither would I. Marriage is what holds this whole world together, sweetie, and don't you forget it, and plenty of women wouldn't have done what they did without getting help from a man, believe me. That Madame Curie got plenty of help from her husband when she was discovering radium, if you remember that picture, which I'm sure you don't because you're much too young. And Amelia Earhart, such a beautiful girl, you think if she had a husband he would have let her fly alone and get lost like that? Never in a million years! No sir, every married woman should have a husband to help her, and most of them do, and if you have the right one it's the best thing in the world."

"Here, here," Sam said.

Brenda Fogelman stared at Sam and Sadie for an instant, then pointed a black finger at the door. "Out!" she said, "and don't come back! I don't need interruptions, especially from someone trying to marry me off. Scram!"

"Just a second," Sadie said.

"Out!"

"Listen, I'm just doing a favor for an old friend."

"Do me a favor and leave me alone!"

"Don't holler, and don't fry off the handle. I only want to find a nice man for you, someone to make you happy. Is that a crime?"

"Just get off my case," Brenda said. "Out!"

Sam tugged at Sadie's elbow. "I think she'd like us to leave."

"That message I got," Sadie said. She opened her handbag and took out a card. "Here's where to find me," she said, handing the card to Brenda. "When you calm down a little, we'll talk."

Brenda put the card into the pocket of her coveralls and walked away, back to her work. It was clear that as far as she was concerned, the interview was over.

"Come," Sam said.

Going down six flights of stairs was easier than going up, and they were soon on the sidewalk. "She's some piece of work, that girl," Sam said.

"Did you see that face?" Sadie said, "a beauty in disguise."

Sam's eyebrows raised and met in the middle of his forehead. "Didn't you hear what she said, Sadie? She's not interested."

"Pish-tosh! With the right man she'll be interested."

"Not unless he looked like a piece of metal," Sam said. "Give it up, my love. Throw away her index card and forget it."

"A Shapiro never quits, and neither does a Mrs. Sam Beck," said Sadie. "You know me—I grab a bulb by the horns, stick it in the ground, and make a flower grow."

"That you do," Sam grinned. "Brenda Fogelman— you'd better start buying your trousseau."

Five

Fred Dubin was in a snit. The tall, lean TV director reached across the conference room table and grabbed a glass ashtray. What he wanted to do was throw it at the two women seated opposite him. At Sadie Shapiro, first of all, the primary cause of his headache, or perhaps a bank shot off Sadie and onto the long nose of Maxine Morris. What he did, instead, was light a cigarette and grab a lung full of carcinogens. "Look," he said roughly, "the idea stinks. Okay? That's my honest opinion."

"You've said that about ten times, Fred," Maxine replied. "That's not being constructive."

"All right. I'll say it again. What we have here is another static discussion program, four people sitting around a table and talking their heads off. I mean there is nothing visually interesting about talking heads."

Maxine nodded. "It's boring, yes. But how else are we going to get our message across? All the information . . ."

"Will you give me a chance!" Dubin snapped. "Look," he went on, getting up from his chair and beginning to pace the room, "the whole message we have to get across is fitness and health, and exercise. We have Frank Shorter, the marathon runner. Dr. Martin Shedley, the guru of long-distance runners and a marathon man himself, right? Now I have about ten miles of film of those two guys in action. Plenty of good running stuff—*which we can show as they talk*! Got the picture? We let them talk and say what they damn please about exercise, but we run film over it, which is a damn sight better than those static talking heads." He looked at Sadie whose eyes had blinked at each damn, and snapped, "That's two 'damn's,' forgive me, forgive me."

"Darn is still good," Sadie said, "but I excuse you because you were angry."

"He's always angry," Maxine said. "Okay, Fred, I agree. But what do we do when Sadie speaks? Or Haj Lothar, the man with the exercise classes?"

"Hell and damnation!" Dubin expostulated. "Sorry Sadie, use your so-called imagination, Max! I'll take Sadie out to the park again and shoot her jogging. For this Lothar guy, we'll take a crew up to his exercise class and shoot all his fat ladies doing deep knee bends, or whatever the hell—sorry—he has them do . . ."

Maxine's brow furrowed in concentration. "That's at least two additional days of shooting, Fred. I don't think we have the money for it."

"How did I get into this nickel-and-dime outfit!" Dubin said. "Look, you want a boring show that will put people to sleep?"

"No."

"All right, compromise," Dubin said. "I'll take our best crew and run their as—tails—into the ground, okay? A one-day shoot and I'll get both Sadie and Lothar on tape. How's that?"

Maxine's long fingers drummed on the table top. "We still don't have the money . . ."

Bile rose in Fred Dubin's throat, but he swallowed it down. How he hated taking orders from anyone, even more so from a woman. And when that Shapiro woman was around, he couldn't even curse. "My God, Max," he pleaded, "will you bend a little? Give me a break! A one-day shoot."

"All right," Maxine sighed, "we'll go over budget again. But only one day, Fred. No more . . ."

"Hallelujah!" Dubin's grin spread his moustache across his craggy face. Impulsively, he grabbed Maxine in a hug and kissed the top of her head. Then, for good measure, he kissed Sadie's cheek. "Now we're cooking," he said. "This may not be such a dumb show after all." With a mock salute, he left the room.

Maxine began gathering the papers spread in front of her. "Fred Dubin is my cross to bear," she said to Sadie.

"He's not a bad person," Sadie said. "If he learned to say heck and darn, he'd be all right. And he's very talented, isn't he?"

"That he is," Maxine nodded, "but so overbearing no one wants to work with him. Want to bet his one-day shoot turns into two days, maybe three?"

"But he just said he'd do everything in one day."

"Not exactly," Maxine said. "I made him beg me for one day, and he promised to try to do it all in one day, but he and I both know that's impossible."

"Wait a minute," Sadie said. "You mean he was lying to you?"

"Not exactly, Sadie. Now I know he'll really *try* to do the shooting as fast as he possibly can."

"Or else the budget, what-you-call-it, won't have enough money in it, right?"

"Oh, no," Maxine grinned. "There's plenty of money in the budget. Even for a three-day shoot."

Sadie looked at Maxine, trying to understand the conversation she had just witnessed, and failing. "So you were lying to him, too?"

"Not lying, exactly," Maxine said, "just exchanging. If I gave Fred the go-ahead for a three-day shoot, he'd take a week. And that kind of money we don't have."

Sadie opened and shut her cornflower blue eyes. "I think I'm getting a headache."

"Exactly," Maxine said, "just like everyone else in television. Come to my office and let's talk about your part in the show."

Sadie sat, looking at Maxine. "Now," she said slowly, "do you really want me to come to your office, or does that mean I should go home?"

Maxine threw her head back and laughed. "No," she said, "you I level with." She took Sadie's arm. "Come."

"Listen, Charlie," Fred Dubin was saying to the TV station's manager, "I want off that stupid health program, and pronto. I can't stand it."

"Really, Fred? Gee, I'm surprised," the station manager said. "Maxine Morris just got finished telling me what a wonderful job you're doing."

"Hmph," Dubin snorted, "Max is one of the reasons I want out. She and that Sadie Shapiro, they're driving me up the wall." Dubin put a mock look of despair on his face and stared at the station manager from under his heavy eyebrows. There wasn't a chance in the world that the manager would grant his request, Dubin knew, but that was not what he was after.

"I'm sorry to hear that," the station manager said. "But you're too far along now for me to relieve you, Fred."

"C'mon, Charlie," Dubin said, "I can be replaced."

"Afraid not, Fred. The crew likes you, the principals know you, and Maxine is satisfied. Looks like you'll have to stick with it." He smiled at Dubin and sat back, waiting for the request he knew was coming.

"Okay," Dubin said, "I'll be a good soldier. But I do have some free time, Charlie. Isn't there something else cooking I could pitch in on? Some new show maybe?"

"Could be."

"Like what?"

The manager picked up a yellow pad on which some notes were scrawled. "Let's see . . . There's World Forum, that discussion show on world affairs we're launching . . ."

"Talking heads," Dubin said. "What else?"

"We're planning a show called 'This Week in Business' . . ."

"Don't tell me," Dubin said, "stock tables, market reports, more talking heads. What else?"

"We're thinking about a weekly show on the new art. A kind of survey of what's going on in the art world. New artists, their work, gallery showings . . ."

"Hey, that's all right," Dubin said. Images of colorful paintings surveyed by the television camera's frame popped into his head. Swirls of color in motion, the moving camera focusing on a still life, bright flowers, nudes. "I like it, Charlie."

"Thought you might," the station manager said, having planned to assign Dubin to the new show some three weeks ago, "I warn you, it's very low-budget."

"What isn't around here?"

"You'll have to produce it, too. Just you, a couple of researchers, and a crew, of course."

"I want it."

"Fine," the station manager nodded. "And you'll continue plugging along on 'Fitness and Health,' won't you?"

"No problem."

As he left the office Dubin was congratulating himself. At last, a show he could use his full talents on, with color and movement. He didn't know much about the art world, but he would learn, and he'd start planning the show right away.

Two floors below, Sadie was just entering Maxine Morris' tiny office, now made even smaller by three large floral bouquets on the floor, the desk and the window sill. "Very nice," she said, "is it your birthday or something?"

Maxine sat down behind her desk. "What? Oh, you mean the flowers. No. They're from that idiot with the horse. He just keeps sending them."

It took a few seconds for the connections to click in Sadie's mind. "Michael Newman? He's sending you the flowers?"

"Every day."

"I knew it!" Sadie crowed. "Such a gentleman, so handsome, and a doctor besides. Maxine, you must be thrilled."

"Why should I be thrilled?" Maxine asked, amusement showing in her eyes. "Just because some rich dilettante —plastic surgeon, no less—wants to throw his money away?"

Sadie blinked twice, not believing her ears. "Maxine, he's very interested in you."

"I know that, Sadie," Maxine said evenly. "He telephones every day, too."

"There, you see? I knew it the minute I saw it. Love at first sight, Maxine. A lot of people don't believe in it, but

I do, because I know how crazy love can make even the sanest person. Your heart sends a message to your eyes and your mind stops working. That's the way it happens. I remember when I first saw my Reuben, let him rest, I almost fainted. Almost passed out and fell on the floor he looked so handsome standing there in his uniform."

"He was in the Army?"

"No, a mailman. With a leather pouch so new and shiny you could almost see yourself in it, which I never did because I couldn't take my eyes off his face. And that was the exact same look I noticed on Michael Newman's face when he saw you, cookie—the same!"

"Right," Maxine said. She opened the middle drawer of her desk and took out a yellow pad. "Now, let's talk about what you'll say on the discussion program."

"Don't change the subject when we're talking about love. Tell me why you're running away from him."

"I'm not running away. I'm just not encouraging him."

"For heaven's sake, Maxine, why not? The man is a catch!"

"He's not my type." Maxine shrugged. "The vibes are wrong."

"The *which*?"

"The vibrations, Sadie. His aura, his persona . . ."

"Talk English," Sadie said. "What is all that guff—something to do with astrology?"

"Perhaps." Maxine grinned. "Maybe that too."

"But that's piffle, Maxine! Listen, I got a friend, Lois Berman, supposed to be born under the sign of Cancer and she's never been sick a day in her life! So don't give me astrology, sweetie."

"Look, Sadie, just take my word for it. Michael Newman is not for me. You've already got three people on your matchmaking list—please don't include me."

"Brenda Fogelman, Harry Wald, and Mrs. Mandelbaum are an obligation," Sadie said. "You I'm helping as a friend."

"Well, stop. I don't need romantic complications in my life right now. I'm too busy."

"Too busy for love?" Sadie said, smiling. "There must be another reason."

"You're worse than my mother!" Maxine stared at the small woman who, in a few short months, had become a friend, confidante, and adviser. "All right, here's the truth. Number one, I'm not impressed by men on horse-back. Number two, every doctor I've heard of wants a sweet little stay-at-home wife and that's not me. Three, I don't like the kind of doctor who makes a fortune by shortening women's noses and wiping out crow's-feet. Four, the man is just too sure of himself for my taste. And five . . . I don't think I'm going to tell you any more."

"All this and you never even spent two minutes with the man." Sadie wagged her gray head. "You can't judge a book by its cover, Max, or a man by his horse."

When the telephone rang, Maxine was grateful for the interruption. Until she heard the voice at the other end. "Is this the lovely Maxine Morris?" Michael Newman asked.

"It's you again."

"Me again. I can get us two tickets to the hockey game at the Garden. Dinner before or after?"

"Neither."

"Fine," Newman said imperturbably. "A concert? Broadway show? How about the new Woody Allen film?"

"Nope."

"Just dinner then, you pick the place."

"Not tonight."

"Tomorrow night? Saturday? Just tell me when."

"Look, I'm busy right now."

"So am I. Did today's flowers arrive? How are they?"

"I meant to tell you about that. You're wasting your money, you know."

"No, I'm not," Newman said. "I steal them from patients in the hospital. Doesn't cost me a penny."

"You don't."

"I do. Only from the dead ones, of course—the ones I've killed."

"You kill one a day?" Maxine asked, chuckling.

"Thousands, actually. Look, how about meeting me for a drink after work?"

"Goodbye," Maxine said.

"Speak to you tomorrow," said Michael Newman.

Maxine put the telephone down slowly.

"That was him, right?" Sadie said.

Maxine nodded. "Wasting his time again."

"He's not for you, right?"

"Right."

"So tell me, cookie," Sadie smiled, "why are you blushing?"

Six

Harry Wald was unwrapping tomatoes, taking off the tissue paper that protected them from bruises, and piling them onto a mass display inside the store. He wore a light windbreaker that once might have been clean. There was a tear in the poplin material below the slash pocket on the right side, and the zipper had long since given up the ghost. He thought of it as a "work jacket," something to protect him against the cold, especially when he stood out on the loading dock of the wholesale market at five in the morning. When his Emily was alive, he remembered, she always saw to it that his clothes were cleaned on time. And when a shirt or jacket had seen its day, she would make him throw it away. That was part of what a wife did, that and many other things, but now there was no longer an Emily to look after him, and he had worn this jacket for a year.

"You call these eggplants?" Mrs. Petrullio said. She

squeezed a small purple eggplant between her long fingers. "This is garbage, Wald."

"It's a little early in the season," Wald said. He put the last tomato on the display and turned to his customer. For twenty years Mrs. Petrullio had been calling his produce garbage. It was her way of shopping, as natural to her as saying good morning.

"Garbage," she said, "you should be ashamed to sell such stuff."

"How many pounds?" Wald asked.

"Three," she said, "and ripe ones."

"For you, only the best," he said. Now he was squeezing eggplants, picking the ones that were ripe and unbruised.

"You don't mind my saying, you look terrible," said the old woman. "You look like you're not sleeping." She squeezed an eggplant. "It's hard when you lose someone. Believe me, I know." Sighing a long Italian sigh, she moved to the tomatoes, fingering them. "These won't be ripe until next Christmas."

"A few days on your windowsill," said Wald.

"Four pounds," said Mrs. Petrullio. She took a tissue from her handbag and dabbed at her nose. "You ought to get married again."

"Who'd have me?"

"A woman can get along alone, but with a man . . ." She nodded approval at the tomatoes Wald put on the scale. "Are you looking?"

"I'm looking," Wald put the tomatoes into a brown bag.

"Are you finding?"

"Not yet," Wald said. And maybe not ever. After a woman like Emily, no other one measured up. Even with this party tonight at Sadie Shapiro's, he had no real hope of finding someone.

"These peppers look like my troubles," the woman said, "two pounds."

Wald picked peppers for her, thinking that in another hour or so he'd leave the store and go home. A shave, a shower, maybe a couple of hours sleep. He'd feel better for it. And if there was no one at the party for him, at least he would have met one nice woman, Sadie Shapiro.

At that same instant, far uptown, Doris Mandelbaum stepped out of her shower. She took a large blue bath towel from the rack and rubbed her body hard. In her mind's eye she saw herself already dressed. The black sheath, gold choker, the matching earrings, the exact amount of makeup and eye-liner. And for what? Maybe, maybe, she told herself.

In front of the mirror she opened the bath towel, looking at her body with a critical eye. Sag and droop, and a roll of cellulite that would never go away. Still, not too bad. Exercise had seen to that, and sensible eating.

She put on a terry-cloth robe and moved to the bedroom. A nice long nap now, what Jacob used to call her "beauty sleep." Jacob, she thought as she turned the sheets down, Jacob. The feel of his hand as he sometimes awakened her from that "beauty sleep" by crawling into bed quietly and nestling next to her. Jacob laughing as he covered her face with kisses. Jacob's hand, stroking her skin . . . Tears came and she let them fall.

It looked like a scene of pandemonium bordering on panic, but actually, thanks to Bryna Pernik, the transformation of Sadie's apartment into a setting for a party was going splendidly. Bryna, a bartender, and a waiter moved furniture aside and set up a long buffet table and a bar. The kitchen had long since been organized by Bryna and even now there was a massive turkey cooking in the oven.

54

"Relax, Sadie," Bryna was saying for the tenth time in the last hour, "everything is under control."

"I keep feeling I forgot something."

"That's not your worry, it's mine. You just greet your guests and see they have a good time. The food and drink is my department."

"Ay-yi," Sadie sighed, then kissed the young Hungarian girl on the cheek. "What would I do without you?" she said. "You're so good at this."

"It's my business," Bryna said.

"Ahem!" Sam Beck coughed, trying to get Bryna's attention. Beside Sam stood Abe Farkas, his friend of many years, who resided at the Mount Eden Senior Citizens Hotel in Hollis, Queens. "If you two lovebirds will stop billing and cooing, Abe and I would like to make a fruitcake report."

"You don't have to tell me," Bryna said, her dark eyes flashing. "The flavor is all wrong, right?"

"Too much cinnamon, I think," said Abe Farkas.

"Too much something," Sam said.

Bryna mumbled a few words in Hungarian. "Nineteen versions of that cake I made, and none of them right," she said. "Thank you very much, grandmother of mine." Turning to Sadie she said, "I went to her apartment again to beg her for the recipe. You know what she told me? If I asked her for it again she'd stop talking to me. Imagine!"

"Take it easy, Bryna," Sadie said, noting the spots of high color in the young girl's cheeks. "It doesn't pay to get excited for a fruitcake."

"Right," Sam nodded, "only for strudel."

Bryna grinned. "Okay, you're right. Now let's go over the guest list again. How many people are coming by the last count?"

"Twenty," Sadie said.

"Thirty," Sam said at almost the same instant.

Bryna looked from Sadie to Sam and back again. "Which is it? Twenty or thirty?"

"I got twenty people on my list," Sadie said. "All the single people from my TV show, from my book publisher, and others I know and they know."

"And I got thirty on my list," Sam said. "All of them relatives and friends of people from Mount Eden that Abe Farkas rounded up."

Bryna, Sam and Sadie stood for a moment, looking at each other. "I think we got trouble," Sam said.

"What's the total number coming?" Bryna asked. She was almost afraid of the answer that was coming.

"How did you get thirty single people, Abe?" Sadie asked. "I thought you'd find five, maybe ten . . ."

Abe Farkas, the former wizard of dry goods, ran a nervous finger inside his white on white shirt collar. "It was like a bombshell out there, Sadie. A matchmaking party for single or divorced people in their fifties. I put a notice on the bulletin board, Mildred Futterman and Bessie Frankel went to work, and everybody knew somebody who had somebody looking to get married. So I invited them all, like Sam wanted me to."

"So we don't have thirty then," Bryna said, "we've got *fifty!*"

"Maybe more," Abe Farkas said in a very small voice. "They were still inviting people when I left."

"Oh, my God!" Sam said.

"Don't panic!" said Bryna Pernik in a shrill voice. "Thank heavens we still have a few hours until the first guests arrive. I'll cope—I don't know how, but I will." She turned on her heel and fled down the hall to her apartment, thoughts of doubling the amount of liquor, wines, mixers and food filling her head.

"There's still something bothering me," Sadie said.

"One of the main guests is not coming, Brenda Fogelman."

"Forget Brenda Fogelman," said Sam, "she's married to metal."

"I could have tried harder to get her here," Sadie said. "Maybe paid her another visit. Hey, wait a minute—"

"No," Sam said firmly. "There's no time to go dashing down there now. Forget it, Sadie."

"I'll still have to do something about that girl," Sadie said.

"You want to make her happy, buy her a new welding torch," Sam said. "A husband you'll never get her." Seeing the distracted look on Sadie's face, Sam squeezed her arm. "What else is worrying you?"

"Harry Wald and Doris Mandelbaum. With so many extra people coming I hope I'll be able to find them in the mob scene."

"You will, don't worry," Sam said. "And they'll both love you, and listen to you, and you'll find them each a husband and wife, and we'll all live happily ever after. Okay?"

"From your mouth to God's ears," Sadie said.

"That's fine with me," Sam said. He turned to Abe Farkas. "And now, my little chickadee," he said, "I think it's time to taste a bit of the grape. What do you say, kiddo?"

"Do I ever say no to schnapps?"

"Good," said Sam. He took his old friend by the arm and led him across the room. "The bar is now officially open," he declared. "Let's get this party on the road."

Seven

The first guest rang Sadie's doorbell a full half hour before eight o'clock. "Am I too early?" she inquired of Sam, and launched into a recitation of the difficulties of *shlepping* to Manhattan via public transportation from the wilds of Plainfield, New Jersey. "We couldn't have started without you," Sam told her, straight-faced, as he led her to the bar for a drink. Her name was Hazel Tishcoff, age fifty, a divorcee whose ex-husband was in Morocco. "The skins, not the place," she explained, "he imports."

By half past eight the living room was filled, and a fog of nervousness filled the air, with men straightening ties and women patting each last hair into place. Strangers among strangers, they behaved like teenagers at a first dance. Men talked to men, women to women, and hardly anyone talked at all until they had a cold, wet glass in hand. But soon there was nervous laughter and loud conversation, and by the time Augie Donatello struck up "Lady of Spain" on his accordion the party was rolling merrily along.

Sadie was having a wonderful time. Wearing a bright paisley knit dress of her own design and manufacture, she moved through the room enjoying herself. A celebrity at large on her own home grounds, she was well-known to most of the guests. She exchanged hugs and pecks on the cheek with many women, including a large lady from Ozone Park who was wearing a dress she had knitted from instructions in Sadie's first knitting book. And it took the combined efforts of Sam and Abe Farkas to rescue her from the clutches of a small birdlike woman whose bony fingers kept picking at Sadie's dress while she demanded complete knitting instructions on the spot.

Sam handed Sadie a glass. "Wet your whistle," he said, "and relax a little. The party is going great."

Sadie sipped. "Two cents plain," she said, "thanks."

"Happens to be Perrier water with a slice of lime," Sam said, "not seltzer. Very fashionable."

"What fashionable?" Sadie said. "My father used to drink this sitting at home in his undershirt."

"This is classy," Sam insisted. "Drink enough and you start belching with a French accent."

Sadie's eyes scanned the room. "I wish Doris Mandelbaum and Mister Wald would show up. They're the reason for this whole party."

At that moment the front door opened and Sadie saw Maxine Morris enter, accompanied by Fred Dubin. They were by far the youngest people in the room, and Maxine made her way to Sadie's side. "What a bash! Sadie, I didn't think you'd have so many people."

"Neither did I," Sadie grinned, "so what if people are belly button to belly button? With all this closeness

59

maybe one couple will click and then it will all be worthwhile."

"Spoken like a true matchmaker," Maxine said. "I'll only stay for a few minutes and then get out of your hair."

"Oh, no, Maxine!" Sadie protested. "You got to stay, please!"

The pleading note in Sadie's voice was not one that Maxine had heard before. "All right," she said, "if it's that important, I'll stay a bit."

"Don't make a move," Sadie said mysteriously, and turned away into the crowd.

Near the bar, Sam Beck was admiring Fred Dubin's tweed jacket. In fact, he was feeling the sleeve. "Beautiful piece of goods," he said.

"This old rag?" Dubin said. "It's about ten years old, Sam."

"When you buy good, it lasts," Sam said.

"Excuse me," a small voice at Sam's elbow said. Sam turned to look and saw a slightly built man, in his fifties perhaps, with thinning gray hair. "Harry Wald," the man said.

"You made it!" Sam beamed. He pumped Wald's small hand and looked him over more carefully. An honest face, sad-looking brown eyes, and clothes that might have been in fashion ten years ago. Wald's suit was a three-button plaid number, with narrow lapels, and the tie was not quite appropriate with it. His shirt was white and clean, which, Sam decided, was about the best thing you could say about it.

"I've got to dash," Dubin said. "Lovely party, Sam. Good luck."

"And good luck on your new show," Sam said.

"Thanks," Dubin grinned, and fighting his way like a

halfback in traffic he disappeared in the direction of the door.

"Come, have a drink," Sam said to Wald, "tell me about yourself." He moved the smaller man to the bar, put a rye and ginger ale in his hand and took another scotch for himself. Sam clinked his glass against Wald's and raised it in a toast. "Here's to you—can I call you Harry?—one of our guests of honor."

"*L'chaim*," Wald said, taking a sip of his drink.

Wald's voice was so low pitched Sam had to strain to hear him. "In the fruit business, right?" he said.

"Right, more than forty years."

"My father was in that business once," Sam said. "Had a horse and wagon."

"So did my father," Wald said. "In Brooklyn?"

"Worked out of the old Wallabout Market in Williamsburg."

"How do you like that?" Wald said, smiling. "So did mine."

Sam clinked his glass against Wald's again. "*Landsman!*"

"And I'm still in that business," Wald said. "I don't know, I guess it suits me."

"How long were you married?" Sam asked.

"Not long enough," Wald said. "I've got a son in California, and another in Michigan, three grandchildren . . ."

"All gorgeous and very smart," Sam said.

"Of course."

Wald looked down at the floor for a moment. Sam took another pull on his cigar. A plain guy, he decided, honest, nice, keeping his head above water, like a million others in this city. "How long has it been?" Sam asked softly.

"Two years," Wald said. He gave a small sigh. "Two very long years."

"This I know about, too," Sam said. "Took me a lot of years to get over losing my first wife, believe me. And then I met that little person who knits—couldn't be more different than my Dora—and the whole world lit up for me again."

"I should be so lucky," Wald said.

Across the room, Maxine Morris felt a hand touch her sleeve and a voice she was now used to hearing say hello. "You!" she gasped, seeing the man who had materialized at her side.

"Me," Michael Newman grinned.

"But how . . .?" Maxine sputtered.

"A little bird told me you'd be here," Newman said.

"A Sadie Shapiro bird," Maxine said. "That *woman!*"

"Is wonderful," Newman said, "and so are you." He took Maxine's hand and held it firmly in his own. Looking at her, he realized that he must be grinning like an idiot. And that feeling he had upon first seeing her in the park returned: a hammering in his heart, a slight loss of breath, the sense that there might be a halo shining behind her auburn hair. Caring about nothing, he smiled on.

"You cooked this up, the two of you. I'll murder Sadie."

"No, you won't," Newman said. "She told me you'd be here, that's true, and of course, here I am. My God, that dress looks wonderful on you and your hair is marvelous —and I think I love you, Max."

The intense look on the young doctor's face, his glassy-eyed stare into her own eyes, put Maxine on her guard. "Slow down, Newman, you're way ahead of yourself," she said.

"But I never felt this way . . ."

"I've heard that before," Maxine said. "Look, take it easy, okay? You don't know a single thing about me, so let's not start talking about love."

Newman took a breath and slowed his heart. "You're twenty-eight, single, never been married, not living with anyone, born in Mount Vernon, New York, April 19th, father is a retired professor of English at Oberlin College, mother, Ida, worked for the Red Cross, you graduated magna cum laude from New York University six years ago, worked as a 'gofer' at NBC, assistant producer at CBS, your favorite color is blue and you're going to marry me."

"You're crazy," Maxine said.

"About you, yes."

"And you've been spying on me."

"Sadie helped, you'd be surprised how much she knows about you. And the rest I found out on my own. Ask me why."

Maxine pursed her lips and half smiled. "Why?"

"Because you're the most important thing that ever happened to me," Michael said.

In spite of herself, Maxine giggled. Michael Newman was very good-looking, and persuasive when he wanted to be. His brown eyes looked soft and vulnerable, his smile warm. She didn't want to be rude, or go out of her way to hurt him, but she felt nothing more than a faint interest in this man who obviously felt much more for her. "Newman," she said, "I could use another drink."

A woman wearing a black sheath dress touched Sadie Shapiro on the arm. "You're Sadie Shapiro, aren't you?"

"Yes."

"Doris Mandelbaum."

"Hello, hello!" Sadie beamed. "I've been waiting for you to come along. Look at you!" Sadie said with a sharp intake of breath. "A beauty!" She held Doris's hand in her own and stepped back to admire her. "A face sweet like sugar and a figure to match." And with that, Sadie pecked Doris Mandelbaum on the cheek. "Such a good-looking woman, my best friends should have your shape. And I love the way you did your hair, and your dress, and that necklace, perfect!"

In spite of herself, Doris Mandelbaum began to blush under Sadie's uncritical gaze and the warm tribute to her looks. No one had complimented her in this fashion in years, not since her mother had passed away, and even Jacob had not been so unstinting in his praise. "Please," Doris said, "you're embarrassing me. In front of all these people . . ."

"Don't be a blushing varlet," Sadie went on. "I'm only saying what anyone with eyes in her head can see. You're having trouble finding a husband? *Um-possible!* Either men have gone blind or you've been hiding your looks under a bushel, and the rest of you as well."

"Thank you," Doris said.

"So how come you're not married?" Sadie asked. "It says on my little card I got from the matchmaker, let her rest, that she sent at least a dozen men to see you. Is it true?"

"That she did. Plenty of men."

"But nothing clicked, right?"

"Here I am," Doris said with a smile. "I don't know, maybe it's still too soon after Jacob. I look at them, I talk to them, I go out with them, but . . ."

"This you don't have to tell me," Sadie said. "I also lost a near and dear, and the pain goes on and on. You had a happy marriage, I can tell."

"As close to perfect as it could be."

"Of course," Sadie nodded. "If it was bad, you wouldn't want any part of another man. When you're happy in a marriage it's the best that life can be. The state of happy matrimony, it's a better state than California or New Jersey or any of them, believe me."

"So where is he?" Doris asked, smiling gently.

"He's living somewhere," Sadie said, "we just have to find him and introduce you. You mustn't give up hope, though, you got to believe it's going to be. I never thought, after my dear Reuben passed away, that I would ever marry again. But Sam came along, and I got used to his ways, and it made me crazy when he wasn't around, and pretty soon I knew that I wanted to be with him forever, or as long as God gives us, because he makes every day a little sweeter. This is what I wish for you."

"And what I wish for myself."

"Tell me about what kind of man I should find for you," Sadie said. "I read what was on your little card, but I want to know more."

Doris raised her shoulders in a shrug. To Sadie's eyes, she seemed embarrassed again. "Like Jacob. Quiet, gentle, but with a kind of inner strength. It would be nice if we shared the same interests. Books, the theater, music . . ."

"What about money?" Sadie said. "It said on your card you were very interested that the man should have money."

"I'm a woman alone, Sadie," Doris said. "I've got enough to live the rest of my life very nicely."

"Which means . . .?"

"I've got to be sensible. I don't want someone who only wants me for my money."

"Of course not," Sadie said. "Wouldn't introduce you to a money-hunter or a fortune-grabber. But Doris, there are a lot of wonderful men who don't have a lot of money . . . and some of them, who knows? One of them could be your Mister Perfect."

"I don't think so."

"Hey—wait a minute," Sadie protested, "most of the immediate world isn't living on Park Avenue. You're leaving out a lot of people, Doris."

"And I couldn't be comfortable with a poor man, Sadie, I know it. Sooner or later, I'd start to wonder—is it me, or is it my money? That's what I want to avoid."

"All right," Sadie said. "I get the picture. But answer me this, cookie. When I send a nice man to see you what are you going to do . . . ask to look at his bankbook before he takes his hat off?"

"No," Doris said. "You are."

Abe Farkas was having a wonderful time, circulating through the room and acting as Sadie's assistant matchmaker. Cardmaker was more like what the assignment was, in fact, and Abe was busy filling out index cards for all of the men and women who had come to the party. Names, addresses and telephone numbers were easy, as was the kind of partner sought. It was surprising how many said the same thing when asked that question: "a good man," or "a nice woman." (Clark Gable and Betty Grable were also answers to the same question.) And what did people reply when asked their age? Don't ask. Abe, with his eye for truth and encyclopedic knowledge of the worth of a piece of goods, made his own judgments and wrote an encoded figure on each card. All Sadie had to do was add five years to each age and it'd come out about right.

Abe fought his way through the crush and found Sam and Harry Wald near the bar. "Sixty-seven cards I got," Abe told Sam, "and every one wants to get married."

"Good work," Sam said. He caught the bartender's eye and got a Scotch for Farkas. "Drink up, Abe, you did splendid."

Harry Wald looked at Farkas appraisingly. "You must be some lady-killer," he said.

Farkas looked up from his drink. "I don't get you."

"Sixty-seven telephone numbers," Wald said. "You must have a lot of time and a lot of strength."

Abe and Sam began to laugh. "The telephone numbers are for Sadie," Sam said after a moment, "to help with her matchmaking."

"You thought they were for me?" Farkas said, laughing again.

"I'm sorry," Wald said.

"Don't be sorry," Farkas grinned. "That's the biggest compliment I got in ten years."

"Don't give up hope," Sam was saying to Harry Wald as they fought their way across the room, trying to make it to the spot where Sadie was last seen standing with Doris Mandelbaum. "Excuse me."

"Now I know how a salmon feels, swimming upstream," Wald said. He followed closely in Sam's wake. "There must be a hundred people here."

"And no small ones." Standing on his tiptoes, Sam spied Sadie. "Ahah, I see her. We make a right turn at the plaid sport jacket and then we'll be there."

"Good," Wald said. "A couple more people come in and we'll have to start breathing in unison."

"Hello," Sadie called as she saw Sam come into view. "This beautiful person with me is Doris Mandelbaum, *the* Doris Mandelbaum, from the card."

"How do you do," Sam nodded. He stepped aside and made room for the man trailing behind him. "And this is Harry Wald."

"Hello, hello," Sadie bubbled. This is a man looking to meet a wife? she wondered as she took him in. How could he have dressed so poorly on an important occasion like this? "Let me say how happy I am to meet you at last," she said to Wald. "And I'd like to introduce you to Doris, here."

"We've met," Wald said, his eyes locked with Doris Mandelbaum's.

"You have?" Sadie was astonished.

"About a year ago," Doris said.

"Fifteen months if you want to be exact," Harry said. "How are you, Doris?"

"Fine."

"So you know each other?" Sadie asked.

"Yes," Doris said.

"We dated," said Harry. "Only once."

"Which was enough," said Doris.

"I said I was sorry, Doris," Harry said.

"I remember." Doris looked away.

"And I kept calling, but you wouldn't go out again."

"She fixed you up, then?" Sadie asked. "The match-maker, Sarah Barish?"

"Yes," Doris nodded, "Harry was one of the ones she sent to me."

"Look," Harry began, "I know we got off on the wrong foot, but it wasn't nice what you did. I mean, you don't hang up a telephone on a person."

"I couldn't see any point in it," said Doris.

"What did I do?" Harry asked, as much to Sam and Sadie as to Doris. "I took her to a sporting event."

"Is that what it was?" Doris said in a voice sweet as honey.

"All right, it was the fights. Ringside seats at the Garden, they cost a fortune. Thousands of people like fights. How did I know you hated them?"

"Let's not discuss it, all right?" Doris said.

"Why not?" Wald said. "Fifteen months I've been walking around burning up at the way you acted that night. You were like an icicle the minute I walked in the door."

"You were half an hour late."

"Did you ever try to park a car in your neighborhood? It's impossible."

To Sadie's eyes, it looked like an argument was building. "Why don't we get some food?" she said. "Isn't that a good idea?"

But Harry Wald didn't take the hint. He had some things to say to Doris Mandelbaum and nothing could stop him now. "And you hated the restaurant, too, right? One of the best in the city."

"I don't eat seafood. I told you that."

"After we were in there, not before. I'm not a mind reader. All you had to do was tell me, we could have gone someplace else. Instead you sat there and sulked."

"I didn't sulk."

"Looked like it to me. Ten minutes, you never said a word."

"Wrong," Doris said with some heat. "I was upset because that old car of yours broke down."

"What old car?" Wald said, astonished. "A Buick, two years old, that's an old car?" He looked to Sam for confirmation.

"Sounds like you two had a wonderful evening," Sam said.

"And it wasn't a breakdown," Wald continued, "it was a flat tire. It could happen even to a brand-new car. You were very snobby about it."

"Oh, was I?" Doris said meanly. "I sulked and I was snobby. Any other nice things you have to say about me?"

"You're a little spoiled, but otherwise okay," Wald said.

"Thank you." Doris nodded.

"So how about it?"

"How about what?"

"One more chance," Wald said. "We couldn't have another evening like that in a million years. What do you say?"

"I say no. And I also say goodnight." Doris Mandelbaum turned and began to make her way into the wall of people.

"So fast you're running away?" Sadie said. "Stay a while."

"I'll call you," Doris said, before she was lost to view.

"Fantastic woman," Wald said, "fantastic."

"That she is," Sam agreed.

"But not for you, Mister Wald, if you don't mind my saying," Sadie said.

"I don't mind," Wald said easily, "but you're wrong. Look around this room, like I did. Is there anyone here like Doris?"

"She's terrific, I agree," Sadie said, "but she just turned you down."

"Doesn't mean a thing," Wald said.

Sam caught Sadie's attention and rolled his eyes, as if to say that Wald was round the bend. "Listen," she said, "there's a lot of peas in a pond. Doesn't just have to be Doris Mandelbaum."

"Oh, but it does," Wald said. "She's exactly the kind of woman I could marry."

"The kind, yes, but not the actual person," Sadie said.

"Why not?" Wald grinned.

"She doesn't like you from the last picture," Sam said.

"And she doesn't like your car," Sadie added, "or your first date, or how you called her snobby, which is never a good word to say to people, or almost anything about you I can think of right now. I mean, give me a week and maybe I'll think of something about you Doris could like, but out of all the people in the immediate world I don't think you got much of a chance with her."

"Listen," Wald said, "you're just beginning as a matchmaker. You didn't think it was going to be easy, did you?"

Eight

The last guest left the party just after two o'clock in the morning. His name was Harry Wald. After Doris Mandelbaum made her dramatic exit, Harry spent the rest of the party drinking, laughing, and telling stories with Sam and Abe Farkas. Not once had he even looked at another woman.

Now Sam was sitting in the yellow club chair, his tie off, surveying the litter that Bryna's crew was clearing away. Abe Farkas was filling his hollow leg once more. Of all the people Sam had ever bent an elbow with, Farkas could drink more and show it less than any of them. He plopped himself down on the couch, opened his collar button and pulled his tie down a notch. "This was some terrific blowout, kiddo," he said.

Sam crossed one leg over the other and removed a shoe. "The man who invented cocktail parties had no feet," he said. He began massaging his toes. "Six hours standing up, I won't be able to walk for a week."

"Thank God you don't have to," Farkas said. He took a sip of his drink. "That Harry Wald is all right."

"That he is." Sam removed his other shoe and winced as he wiggled his toes.

"I never got to meet that Mandelbaum woman," Farkas said. "What's she like?"

"Classy," said Sam. "Well-spoken, well dressed. A little too classy for Harry, I'm afraid."

"Not according to Harry."

"Now you see the problem." Sam removed one of his socks and looked closely at his foot. "Terminal bunions," he said, "I may never tap dance again."

"Harry's going to go after that Mandelbaum woman," Farkas said. "She's number one on his hit parade."

"He'll have as much luck as I did with Elizabeth Taylor," Sam said.

"I wouldn't be too sure," Farkas said. "He likes her a lot."

"It takes two to tango, or even foxtrot," Sam said. "How do you tell a guy he's banging his head against the wall? Harry is a nice guy, but he's not for Doris Mandelbaum."

In the kitchen, Sadie sat having a cup of tea with Bryna Pernik. "Are you sure you don't want a piece of fruitcake?" the young woman asked. "I could slip right down the hall to my place and bring you back a piece."

"Is it any good?"

"No."

"Then I'll just have the tea, thank you very much. And also I have to thank you for doing such a wonderful job tonight. The food was terrific and I think everybody enjoyed everything."

"I'll tell you what I enjoyed," said Bryna, "Michael Newman. Wow, what a gorgeous hunk of man."

"And a doctor, don't forget."

"Who's forgetting? He can put his stethoscope on me anytime."

"Bryna!" Sadie said, acting slightly scandalized, "behave yourself. Michael Newman happens to be in love with Maxine. The man is crazy about her."

"And she's just plain crazy," Bryna said. "Why is she giving the poor guy such a hard time?"

"Who knows?" Sadie shrugged, "especially with love. Love can drive even a sane person crazy. But sometimes one man's mate is another man's person. And vice versa, if you get my drift, which I see you don't because you're looking at me in a funny way."

"It could be that he's just not Maxine's type, Sadie."

"Type-shmipe, let her get to know him a little bit, give the man a chance. That's why I made sure they would meet here tonight. And I was very glad to see them leave together. I mean, they could be together right now for all I know."

Had Sadie Shapiro been able to see what was taking place at that very moment in an apartment closer to midtown, she would not have been surprised. Michael Newman was floating somewhere south of Eden, his arms about Maxine, his lips pressed on hers, his mind in the limbo of lovers. He had taken Maxine from the party to a popular East Side restaurant where they each had one of the most expensive hamburgers known to man. From there, a short drive along the parkway to just north of the George Washington Bridge where they had parked and talked for an hour while watching the moon shining on the Hudson. Now they were in Maxine's two and a half room flat, on her couch to be exact.

Maxine came up for air. She put a gentle hand on Michael's chest and gave herself breathing room. "Newman," she said, "take a break."

"Why a break?" Michael murmured. "This isn't work." He planted the tiniest of kisses on the end of Max's delicious nose, then released her from his arms.

Maxine shifted her position on the couch, tucking her legs up under herself and smoothing her skirt over them. She patted her hair back into place. "As I was saying before I was so nicely interrupted, this is not going to work."

"There you go with work again," Michael grinned. "This is pleasure, Max, a whole different thing."

"Be serious, Michael. I mean it."

"Okay, serious." Michael sat up straight, folded his hands in his lap, the mock student at his schoolroom desk. "Proceed."

"You're still not serious. Will you wipe that silly grin off your face?"

"Aye, aye, sir," Michael said between gritted teeth. "Grin gone."

Maxine giggled, then shook her head. "You are a very silly person, Michael. Especially for a doctor."

"Doctor is in love, making him crazy," Michael said without moving his lips or smiling. "Proceed."

"Well, I am not in love with you—repeat, not."

"Soon will be," said Michael; "proceed."

"You want to get married and I don't. It's as simple as that."

"Can't we go back to kissing, Max? I liked that better."

"No, you goose," Maxine said. "Look, you're a very nice person, I like you a lot, okay? But I know in my heart that's as far as it's going to go, Michael. You told me before—you're thirty, you want to settle down, get married, have children . . ."

"We could have the children first and then get married, but my mother would be very upset."

". . . and I, on the other hand, do not—repeat not—

74

want to get married. Not now. I'm right at the beginning of something good in my career. I work practically all the time. I don't have room in my life for someone like you. I can't give you the time you want and should have. It's just unfair of me to string you along on that. My work comes first."

"Marry me," Michael said. "It'll be all right."

"You keep saying that," said Maxine. She reached over to the end table behind the couch and picked up her cigarettes.

"Of course I keep saying that. It's what I want."

Maxine lit a cigarette and took a long puff. "Look, I almost married a doctor five years ago. I went into Mount Sinai to have a polyp removed and came out with this . . . *growth* attached to me named Stanley Goodman. He wouldn't let me out of his sight for six months. I didn't love him, either, and when he gave me this huge ring I had to break it off between us."

"You broke his ring?" said Michael with a straight face.

Maxine giggled again, then punched Michael's arm gently. "I know all about doctors," she said. "Every one a prince. Office hours, two to four, hospital rounds in the morning, dinner on the table at six every night. Your life is too orderly, you run everything by the clock. And talking to you right now is a woman whose life is a shambles —complete disarray—I don't know from one day to the next what my schedule is going to be. *And I like it that way.*"

"Listen, Max, I can be just as disorganized as the next person."

"But you're not, don't you see? You ride your horse at the same time each day—you told me so yourself—and you have office hours and an operating schedule. I'm just the opposite. I like to spend rainy Sundays reading the paper in my pajamas, staying up till three in the morning to finish a good book, blowing a whole Saturday by going to three movies in a row and eating nothing but popcorn. Now you're not like that, are you?"

"I want you, Max," Michael said, "and just the way you are."

"You don't, Michael, I know you don't. Sooner or later, if we got together, you'd start to organize me and that would be the end. I'd start to be guilty about what I do, I'd have to give up my dreams, my hopes, and I'd become your satellite. And I won't."

"You don't know me at all," Michael said. "I'm not that kind of guy, Max. Really, I'm not."

"Sooner or later, it wouldn't work," Maxine said. "Better let's stop now—before we get all involved."

"Stop, hell," Michael said, moving forward to hold her in his arms again. He kissed her left eye and then her right one. "You have only one flaw," he said, then kissed the tip of her nose. "You talk too much." So saying, he closed her mouth with his own in a most satisfactory way.

Nine

"Two minutes to tape!" a disembodied voice called through the television studio.

"So what happened with you and Michael?" Sadie was asking a very nervous Maxine Morris. Sadie was dressed in her favorite pink hand-knitted sweat suit, with a baby blue scarf about her neck for color. As she spoke to Maxine a makeup woman was applying a thin coat of orange pancake to her forehead.

"Never mind what happened," Maxine said. "Are you ready to tape this spot?"

"Of course. But first you have to tell me about Michael. Don't think I didn't see the two of you leave together. So what happened, cookie?"

"It was very nice," Maxine said.

"Good. And . . . ?"

"And very personal . . ."

"Excellent!" Sadie grinned. "Personal is the best way

to be. Did you two get lovey-dovey right away, or what?"

"Sadie!" Maxine was beginning to blush.

"Ahah! I knew it!"

"One minute to tape!" the voice cried.

"Knowing him," Sadie went on, "he probably proposed to you already. Am I right?"

"You're a witch!" Maxine said. "What did you do, bug my couch?"

"And you said yes, of course."

"Sadie, we have a show to do."

"Show, shmow—love is more important. So did you say okay? What happened, Maxine?"

"Stand by! Ten seconds to tape!"

Maxine ran from the set and into the control booth. As the countdown ended and the cameras came up on line, she was in her chair.

"Cue music!" Fred Dubin ordered, and the show's perky theme was heard in the booth. Dubin let it play for twenty seconds as camera number one focused on the credit crawl. "Stand by, Sadie!" he said, then, "Cue Sadie!"

Outside, the floor manager pointed a heavy finger and Sadie began to talk.

"Hello, it's me again, Sadie Shapiro, the jogging lady, talking to all of you but especially people over sixty-five.

"I'm talking exercise, taking care of your body so it can take care of you. Now a lot of you don't know from exercise, and keeping fit and trim. Lots and lots of people over sixty-five, what they think is that taking out the garbage is enough exercise. Or moving from their chair to the TV set and back.

"Couldn't be more wrong.

"The body is a machine. With a lot of working parts, we should all be so lucky. And if you don't exercise that machine and let it do some work for a change, you're going to wind up with your machine in the garage for repairs.

"You know about the garage for the body? It's called a hospital.

"Okay, let's talk jogging, which is what I know about. I started jogging twenty-five years ago. On a Tuesday in September. When I began jogging around my neighborhood it wasn't like it is today, where you see people out jogging all the time. In those days, people thought I was some kind of nut case. But now we know that jogging is terrific exercise for your heart and your lungs and your liver and God knows what else inside you. It's also a wonderful thing for your mind, which nobody talks about, but it's true anyway. Get your body feeling good and your mind will follow along. What else can it do, stand there?

"We've got a little film of me jogging through Central Park. I'd like you to look and see how I do it, while I tell you some more. Okay? Let's see the film . . ."

"Cue film!" said Fred Dubin up in the control booth. He looked at his stop watch and grinned. "What a pro! She hit that cue right on the second."

"She's amazing," Maxine agreed.

"I think she's some kind of doll," Dubin said. "Wind her up and she starts talking."

". . . And another thing," Sadie was saying.

Doris Mandelbaum was just about to prepare her lunch when the apartment house intercom buzzed. She walked to the front door speaker off the foyer. "Man here with a package for you, Mrs. Mandelbaum," the doorman said. "I'll bring it up."

A few minutes later he was handing her a large basket of fruit.

She brought it to the kitchen, placed it down on the

table. Mystified, she searched for a card. Between a Golden Delicious apple and a large tangerine there was a wrinkled piece of paper. She unfolded it and read: "Terrific seeing you the other night. I'll be calling. Meanwhile, have a piece of fruit." It was signed, Harry Wald.

In spite of her feelings about the man, Doris found herself smiling. She had not had a gift from a man, even a paltry basket of fruit, in a long time. It felt good. She looked at the fruit basket. It was so like Harry Wald, what little she knew of him. The basket was clean, well ordered and packed, but the note was scribbled on a smudged and wrinkled piece of paper. That was probably a good indication of the man.

Two hours later she was reading a book when the phone rang. "Doris? Did you get the basket?" Harry Wald asked.

"Yes."

"Ah, good. I was afraid maybe it didn't get there yet. I sent this guy who works for me, he's not the most reliable."

"I have it, and thank you."

"You're welcome," Harry said. There was a long pause. Harry thought of three things to say and said none of them. He spoke again, "What happened was, I got these tangelos in this morning. From Arizona. Very special, these tangelos, so I thought of you right away."

"Harry . . ." Doris began.

"What I mean is—your usual tangelo is an Orlando, that's what most people grow, you see. Or some of them grow Minneolas. Down in Florida. But these are Sampson tangelos, the sweetest variety. Believe me, you don't see them in New York too often."

"Well, thanks again," Doris said.

Harry paused again. He was surprised at how nervous

he felt. Doris sounded cold and distant. Her voice gave him nothing. "The grapefruits are special, too," he said miserably, knowing as he spoke the words that it was not at all what he meant to say, or indeed, what he should be talking about. "They're Thompsons, pink and sweet. Some people think the Rubys are better grapefruits, but I always found them not as tasty . . . as the Thompsons, I mean." God, you sound like a moron, Harry thought to himself.

"I'm sure they're very nice," Doris said.

Idiot! Harry mentally kicked himself. "Listen, Doris," he blurted out, "I wish they were diamonds!"

"Harry," Doris interjected, "don't . . ."

"Honest to God, Doris, I do. I've been thinking about you since we met again. There's something about you. . . . I mean . . ."

"Harry, I'm going to hang up in a minute."

"Doris, please, give me a chance, will you? Hanging up is not nice. I'm talking honestly to you, saying what's on my mind. You can't shoot me for that."

"I don't want to shoot you," Doris said.

"So listen, then. Give a guy a second chance."

"It's senseless."

"Not for me, it's not. Look, there's a concert next Saturday at Lincoln Center. Tchaikovsky. Do you like him? And afterward we could go eat somewhere. This time *you* pick the place. Anywhere, Doris."

"Harry, no," Doris said firmly.

"Why not?" Harry said. "Are you busy—or what?" He waited a moment, and when she didn't speak, went on. "I promise you, it won't be like last time. My God, it couldn't be like that again. And what's the worst that could happen? You'd spend another evening with me. Am I so bad? I mean, really? So what do you say?"

"Harry, I'm sorry."

"Doris, please. Listen, I never begged a woman in my life, but if that's what you want, I'll beg."

"Now you listen to me, Harry Wald. Just because you send me a basket of fruit, which was very sweet of you, that doesn't mean I owe you a thing. I'm saying I won't go out with you because I just don't want to."

"But why?"

"Harry, don't make this difficult."

"It's already difficult. I'm standing here like a sixteen-year-old, shaking in my boots. Tell me why you hate me."

"I don't hate you."

"I don't hate you either. In fact, I'm beginning to be crazy about you. Of all the women I've met in the past couple of years, you got something none of them has . . ."

"I don't want to hear this . . ."

"The way you hold yourself, Doris, the way you move. The way you talk, even when you're turning me down . . ."

"Harry, goodbye. I'm hanging up." Doris took the receiver away from her ear and placed it on its cradle.

"I'll call you again," Harry Wald said, but no one was listening.

Ten

Fred Dubin was whistling as he walked along the dirty street in lower Manhattan. The director and producer of the upcoming television show "This Week in Art" was finding the tracking down and interviewing of new young artists a welcome relief from his chores on the exercise show featuring Sadie Shapiro. The art show got him out of the studio, for one thing, away from the ingrown atmosphere of station procedure and politics. And he was beginning to have an appreciation of the new and varied work he was seeing. Some of it was worthless, of course, and a lot of it was sophomoric and, worse, pretentious. But now and then he would see something worthwhile, something fresh and alive, and that was what gave appetite to his searching.

He looked at the number of the building, checked the note in his hand, then took the steps two at a time. He strode down a dark hallway and thrust his head inside the offices of an electrical supply firm. "Brenda Fogelman? Is she in this building?"

The clerk behind the counter did not look up from his newspaper. "The weirdo on the top floor."

Dubin started the long climb. The lanky director was in good physical condition, but even he was winded by the time he reached the sixth floor. The sound of a heavy hammer beating on metal led him to Brenda Fogelman's studio. He knocked twice, waited for a reply, and when none came he opened the black door and walked in. After several weeks of visiting artists at their work places he was somewhat used to the unkempt and seedy air he had found, but the sight of Brenda Fogelman's littered studio shocked him.

A figure dressed in dirty denim overalls and a plaid flannel shirt was bent over a low workstand, hammering a piece of brass.

"Brenda Fogelman?" Dubin called out.

The figure straightened up, looked in Dubin's direction, and pushed a pair of goggles away from her eyes. "What the hell do you want?" Brenda said. "Can't you see I'm working?"

"You *are* Brenda Fogelman?"

"No, I'm the Queen of Sheba." Brenda lowered her goggles and turned back to her hammering, as if Fred Dubin did not exist.

Dubin was amused. He had seen artists' temperament before, indeed, he had an ample supply of it in his own character. Stepping carefully around and over the detritus on the floor, he approached Brenda Fogelman.

"You still here?" she said, looking up. And then she unleashed a string of obscenities and oaths that can be heard at most truck stops in Kentucky.

Dubin listened patiently, until Brenda ran out of words. Then, to the young girl's surprise, he calmly threw back at her his own pet assortment of curses, some picked up in Liverpool and Marseilles, and most of them obviously unknown to Brenda, judging by the look on her face. "Okay," Dubin said, "now we're even. Unless you want to start another round?" He wrinkled his nose and sniffed the air. "My God," he said, "don't you ever bathe?"

"What's it to you?"

"You offend my nose," Dubin said. "But, no matter. In pursuit of art all things are possible."

Brenda put her hammer down, turning aside thoughts of braining this tall, well-dressed stranger whose craggy face was oddly attractive. "Who the hell are you?"

"Fred Dubin."

"Never heard of you."

"Ah, but I have heard of you." He told her about the gallery owner he had seen, the one who was preparing the show of Brenda's work, and how the man had recommended that he come and see her. As he talked, Brenda listened, her eyes taking in the tailored corduroy jacket with the leather-patched sleeves Dubin was wearing, his whip-cord slacks and brass belt buckle, the bright gleam of his boots. But mostly she looked into Dubin's slate-gray eyes, the dark slash of his wide moustache, the rough slant of his generous and strong nose. "And that's why I'm here, to take a look at your work, my dear."

"God damn it, I hate interruptions," Brenda said. Another curse came to her tongue, but she checked it, wondering even as she did, why this Dubin was having such an odd effect on her.

"Get used to it," Dubin said. "New York is not a monastery, and you live in the real world, even though you may be an artist. Consider it a part of your work."

"Now look," Brenda said, almost by rote, "I don't need this and I don't need you."

"Oh, no?" Dubin said calmly. "Perhaps not. But if I do

get a look at your work, and if I do like it, then maybe—just maybe—I can help you. In one night, on my television show, I can present your work to hundreds of thousands of people. You do hope to let people look at your sculpture eventually, don't you?"

Brenda nodded.

"Excellent, that's a start, anyway. Now where is your work?"

Brenda stared at Dubin for a moment, caught up in the spell of his voice and the authority he carried with him. Silently, she led him across the studio and pointed out her finished sculptures.

Dubin took a long time inspecting them. They were fresh and interesting, no better and no worse than many he had recently seen. A few showed real insight and talent. The girl was by no means a great artist, he judged, but she was an original. He looked away from the work and stared at Brenda. She had an interesting face, complete with dirty smudges across her cheek. In her eyes there was an intelligence reflected, and something else—a kind of liberated female look. Brenda Fogelman was her own woman, without doubt. Dubin took her arm and led her toward her work.

"What do you want?" Brenda asked.

"Stand behind your work for a moment."

"What for?"

"Just do as I say, there's a good girl."

"Woman, you mean, good *woman*," Brenda said.

"My dear woman, I never doubted it. Now, please, shut up."

Dubin took a few paces back and brought his hands up to frame the picture he had in his mind. Shapes and images floated, the dirty, unkempt girl and her shining metal sculpture, beauty in the work and not in the artist. He saw colors now, and camera movement. Yes, it was good. He could do an entire show on Brenda Fogelman and her work. No, better still—he could cover the opening of her exhibition at the gallery. Yes, that was better. Well-dressed people crowding around this unkempt *artiste*, the clean lines of her sculpture making a statement of the New York artist's world.

"Listen, Dubin," Brenda said, "who are you, anyway? Tell me about yourself."

"For heaven's sake, why?"

Brenda looked at her work boots. Words did not come. "I don't know," she shrugged. "You interest me."

"Let's keep this professional and not personal, shall we?"

"Are you married?" Brenda asked.

"Certainly not."

"Living with someone?"

"Not at the moment."

"Oh, God!" Brenda blurted as the thought struck her, "you're not gay, are you?"

"What?" Dubin said, laughing. "No, not gay—just happy."

"Good," Brenda nodded, "good."

Dubin looked at her shrewdly and shook his head. "I'm not interested in you that way. But I do like your work."

For the first time in five years, Brenda used a word she had almost forgotten. "Thanks."

"Don't thank me now," Dubin said, "wait. Brenda, my dear, I think I'm going to make you a star."

Eleven

"Come on now, be nice," Sam Beck was saying to the crossword puzzle of *The New York Times*. He had sailed through the upper left-hand corner with no trouble at all, then zipped down the middle almost to the bottom. But now they were throwing him a curveball. A four-letter word for a range of mountains in India. Sam took a long pull on his Upmann Special and thought of a few four-letter words he'd like to use on the man who had made up this puzzle. Mountain ranges in India? He knew of the Himalayas, and the female version, the Heralayas. Or were those in Nepal? Tibet, maybe. . . .

When the telephone rang, he was happy for the interruption.

"Sam? This is Harry Wald. Is Sadie there?"

"Hello, Harry. No. Sadie is off in televisionland. What's the problem?"

"Doris Mandelbaum, what else? Listen, I gotta talk to someone. I'm going out of my mind."

"Take it easy."

"The woman won't give me a tumble, Sam."

Sam sighed. Wald's voice carried a note of despair. "Sometimes women get that way."

"I need help. Listen, Sam, can I talk to you?"

"We're talking now."

"Not on the telephone. I mean, can I see you?"

"Sure."

"I'll buy you lunch, okay?"

"Fine," Sam said. "Harry, you wouldn't know a four-letter word for a range of mountains in India, would you?"

There was a short silence. "Kush, the Hindu Kush."

Sam looked down at the puzzle. "Son of a gun, it fits! Thanks, Harry. Do you like Chinese food? There's a good Chinese joint on Broadway."

"Fine," Wald said.

"It's called the Szechuan Hot Pot. I'll meet you there in half an hour."

Thirty-five minutes later, Sam met Wald at the restaurant's door. The fruit merchant was wearing a zip-front jacket that seemed to have defied all the miracle detergents on the market. "Sorry I'm late," Wald said, "the parking is terrible up here."

"Don't worry about it. In fact, you made pretty good time from Brooklyn."

"I wasn't in Brooklyn," Wald said. "I was in my store in Manhattan."

"I see." Sam eyed Wald's jacket. "Who does your clothes, Yves Saint Laurent?"

"What? Oh, this jacket," Wald said.

"Looks like a Salvation Army reject."

Wald grinned at Sam. "I don't pay attention to clothes."

"Obviously."

"I'm not in a white collar business," Wald said. "It's kind of rough and tumble."

"Right," said Sam. "Let's eat." He held the door for Wald, then followed him into the restaurant. "The food is not too bad here, and they leave you alone so we can talk." He led Wald to a booth along the far wall. They seated themselves and Sam caught a waiter's eye. "I usually drink beer with Szechuan food, is that okay?"

Wald nodded.

Sam ordered two bottles of beer. "It's good beer, from the real China. Bottled in Hangchow, or some such place."

"Can I get chow mein here?" Wald asked.

"Not unless you want to insult the chef. Better let me do the ordering. Can you eat hot food?"

Wald shrugged. "I'll take a chance."

"Good," Sam ordered hot-sour soup, spicy eggplant, and a chicken dish called Emperor's Fire. Then he sat back and took a long sip of his beer. "Tell me about Doris Mandelbaum. You sounded very upset on the phone."

"Upset? I'm only going bananas, that's all. She's a hard case, Sam. One bad night we had and now she won't see me again. And meanwhile, I'm walking around like puppy love. I can't get her out of my mind."

"That's tough."

"A man my age with a crush on a woman won't give him the time of day. It's insane!"

"Insane is right," Sam said, "but it could be love, which is sometimes the same thing." He thought for a moment. "Have you dated other women recently?"

"Who wants to?"

"You ought to try, Harry. There are other fish in the sea."

"The heck with fish," the fruiterer said fiercely. "It's Doris or no one."

Sam started to reply, then checked himself when the soup arrived. "Hot-sour soup," he announced, "see if you like it."

Wald picked up a spoon and stirred the thick brown soup. "It doesn't have wontons, does it?"

"No won tons."

"Wontons I like," Wald took a sip of the soup, his eyes widening in surprise as the tart and spicy taste spread through his mouth. Hastily, he took a sip of his beer, then gulped for air. "My God!" he said.

"That's the hot part," Sam said, "the sour you get later." He began eating his own bowl of soup, as Wald watched. "Taste it again," he told Wald, "it grows on you."

"I'll pass on the soup," Wald said. He watched Sam finish his soup while he told him of the affair of the basket of fruit he had sent Doris. "So that's the thanks I get, Sam. She hangs up the phone on me."

"It happens," Sam shrugged. "Maybe you shouldn't have sent her the fruit."

"Why not?" Wald asked. "That was pretty near a twenty-five dollar basket I sent her. Choice stuff, Sam."

"That's not what I meant. I'm sure it was your best. But you're in the fruit business, right? Sometimes people misunderstand when you send them something from your own business. They think it doesn't cost you anything."

"So what should I have sent her?"

"Flowers . . . chocolates, maybe. Sent from a fancy shop. The idea isn't the gift, you know, it's the impression it makes."

"Okay," Wald nodded, "next time she gets flowers." He took a sip of his beer. "My guess is she'll hang up on me again, even if I send her the moon."

A waiter approached the table and set down a tray. He cleared the soup bowls and served the next two courses. Sam uncovered the serving dishes and doled out portions for Wald and himself. "Eggplant and chicken," he told Wald. "Take yourself some white rice and dig in."

"Eggplant I like," Wald said. He spooned some of it onto his plate.

"Be careful, and don't eat those horn-shaped things. They're peppers."

"Hot stuff, eh?"

"Steam will come out of your ears if you even look at them."

Wald surveyed the food with a suspicious eye. Exercising caution, he took a small forkful of eggplant. He chewed a few times, gingerly, then swallowed. Suddenly his eyes grew large and, choking, he grabbed his beer glass and downed it, then hastily drank an entire glass of ice water.

"Isn't this great?" Sam said between mouthfuls.

Tears stood in Wald's eyes. He felt as if someone had scorched his mouth and throat with a blowtorch.

"I love it," Sam said. He served himself another portion of the eggplant. "Wait'll you taste the chicken . . . *fantastic*."

Harry Wald knew he would not live to taste the chicken. Taking Sam's water glass, he drank it down, then filled his mouth with plain boiled white rice. Incredulous, he stared at Sam through tear-filled eyes. "You mean," he gasped, "people actually pay to eat this?"

Sam nodded, his face a picture of bliss.

"This isn't food—it's fire!"

"It is a little hotter than usual."

"Hot, he says." Wald sucked air down his incinerated throat. "Just what I left on my plate could warm Pittsburgh for the winter."

Sam laughed, then signaled the waiter and ordered two more beers. "Would you like something else, Harry?" he asked. "Maybe something not quite so spicy?"

"Who can eat?" Wald shrugged. "I feel like I just had my tonsils removed. Without anesthesia."

"Then you'd better have some ice cream."

"Make it vanilla."

Sam sat back and lit a cigar. What about Harry Wald and the very selective Doris Mandelbaum? He didn't rate the fruiterer more than a ten to one shot to even get a second date with the classy lady in question. And why was that? Sam looked at the faded flannel shirt Wald was wearing under his torn and dirty jacket. And down below, faded olive green khaki pants with a big grease stain on one knee. A picture of sartorial splendor Wald was not. If clothes make the man, Sam thought, then a lack of clothes can certainly unmake him as well. How about that suit Wald wore to the party? It was certainly one of the nicest suits of 1968. No, it would not have been elegant or stylish even back then.

Granted, the retail fruit business was not an occupation for gentlemen. Sam remembered those wild, bygone days on his father's horse and wagon. Rough and tumble, Wald called it. It was that even today. The line of dirt under Wald's fingernails testified to it.

Sam took a long pull on his cigar. But Wald was more than his job. The man was warm, had a sense of humor, he was no dummy. Anyone who can come up with a four-letter Indian mountain range was okay. Kush, indeed.

But Doris Mandelbaum had been married before to a man who obviously was in another league. She had wealth, and was afraid of losing it. And she had already rejected Harry at least three times. Three strikes is out in baseball, and many other games.

"So what should I do about Doris?" Wald asked, even as Sam had the question in his mind.

"Do? I don't know if you can 'do' anything." He looked speculatively at Wald. "Can I speak honestly?"

"Is there another way?"

"I don't want to hurt your feelings, Harry."

"Go ahead," Wald said with a wave, "my feelings have been hurt by the best of them."

"All right, let's take a good look at Harry Wald, the way Doris Mandelbaum sees him, perhaps. Tall enough, still has all his hair . . ."

"Not all," Wald grinned, "but my teeth are my own."

"Face . . . no Gregory Peck, but not a bad-looking guy. Clean shaven if not clean-cut, let's say."

"So far, so good."

"Right," Sam said. "Now let's get to clothing . . ."

"I know what you're going to say and you're right," Wald interrupted. "I've let my wardrobe run down, Sam, and I know it. My suits are old, my shirts are old, I haven't spent anything on clothing since Emily died."

"If you'll excuse me for saying this, Harry, your clothes were not terrific when they were new. Where do you buy your suits?"

Wald named a popular mid-price men's store.

"That's not good enough, Harry, not for Doris. Have you noticed the kind of style she dresses with? You'll have to match that, I'm afraid. You have to look like you belong together when you take her out."

"*If* I ever take her out again," Wald said.

"One other thing about clothes," Sam said. "I realize that you're wearing working clothes. But Harry, if I didn't know you and you came up to me on the street looking the way you do today, I just might hand you a quarter."

Wald nodded, his lips pinched together. "Right, right, right. When Emily was alive, I didn't look like this, believe me." Wald took a felt-tip pen from his pocket and wrote something down on a paper napkin.

"Taking notes?"

Wald nodded.

"You'd better, because I may ask questions later." Sam took a sip of his beer. "The next part is something you have to face. Has it occurred to you that you just might not be Doris's type?"

"That doesn't worry me, Sam."

"Good. There's nothing like confidence. She's a cultured lady, Harry, with refined tastes."

"So am I," Wald said, "or I used to be. Once upon a time I read books, went to concerts, shows, even the opera. With Emily, of course. But these last couple of years . . . I sit in front of the stupid television set and watch any sports show going. Wrestling, even, the roller derby . . ."

"Which is why you took Doris to a prizefight."

"A mistake I'm still paying for," Wald said. "I'm not a stupid guy, Sam, although sometimes it's hard to tell. Hell, I went to college for eight years," he said, smiling, "that's counting four years out in the middle to help Patton win the war. I'm educated, run a pretty successful business, too."

"That you do," Sam agreed, "which brings me to probably your biggest problem. Doris Mandelbaum is a very wealthy widow. She won't have anything to do with a man who might be a fortune hunter." Sam looked directly into Harry Wald's brown eyes.

"I have money."

"Of course, but there's money, and there's money."

"I'm comfortable," Harry said, "believe me."

"I believe you. You've got a fruit store in Brooklyn, and another one in Manhattan you mentioned. With two fruit stores you probably make a pretty good living."

"I don't have *two* fruit stores," Harry Wald said, "I have *forty-eight* of them."

"What?" Sam's cigar almost dropped from his fingers.

"And I own a piece of the wholesale operation up in the Bronx," Wald went on, "plus orange and grapefruit groves in Arizona, California, and Florida. When I say I'm well off, Sam, I mean it."

"But the way you look," Sam said, "the way you live . . ."

"I've never had a problem making money. *Spending* it, that's what I don't know about."

"That you'll learn," Sam said, smiling, "that you can learn."

Twelve

Outside the kitchen window the sun was going down. Inside the kitchen Sam's temper was going up. "So you see, Sadie," he was saying for the third time, "Harry Wald is no *schlemiel*. He's probably got as much money as Doris."

Sadie stood by the kitchen window, practicing the deep breathing exercise she had learned only yesterday. A yogi she had interviewed on the heart and lungs segment of the TV show had demonstrated it for her: take a very deep breath, hold it for ten seconds, then slowly exhale for ten more seconds. It seemed to have done wonders for the yogi, who claimed to be one hundred and twenty years old. "You don't look a day over a hundred and one," Sadie had marveled.

"Thank you," the yogi had said, and imparted the following wisdom in Sadie's ear. "Eat no meat, and drink nothing but orange juice with honey."

"Just my luck," Sadie whispered back, "orange juice gives me terrible heartburn."

"So isn't that terrific about Wald?" Sam said. "Sadie?"

. . . eight, nine, ten, Sadie counted in her head, holding her breath.

"I know you're alive because your face is turning pink," Sam said. "Hello?"

. . . seven, eight, nine, ten, Sadie finished exhaling.

"Listen," Sam said, "if we're going to talk you'll have to stop breathing."

"All right," Sadie said, "finished breathing." Panting a little, she sat down at the table. Before her were the sixty-seven cards Abe Farkas had gathered from the people at the party.

"So what I figure is this," Sam said, "Harry is back in the ball game again. With Doris, that is."

"That would be nice, but I'm not too sure. To Doris, Harry Wald is a lost gauze. Like a bandage that falls off a finger and you throw away."

"He's crazy about her."

"And she can't see him for dust," Sadie said. "So there you are, Mister Anthony, and what do you do now?"

"Listen, I'm only the assistant matchmaker here. You're the boss lady."

"Hoo hah! Some boss. I already called Doris Mandelbaum to ask her to give Harry another chance . . ."

"And . . . ?"

"It was like banging my head on the wall. What a Stonewall Jackson that Doris can be. Wouldn't budge an inch, and if I said two more words I got the feeling she wouldn't talk to *me* again, either."

"Poor Harry. He's going to be very disappointed."

"How about me?" Sadie said, "I'm disappointed, too. The man is a sweet person and he'd be very good for Doris. The same as her first husband, only very different.

What Doris wants is her Jacob all over again and you can't find two people the same in one lifetime, except if one is a Corsican Brother, if you remember that picture, and one of them died in the end anyway."

"Maybe you could talk to Doris again," Sam said.

"And maybe if I grew wheels I could be a trolley car," Sadie countered. "No, I don't think she'd listen to me about Harry Wald. Not even if I told her he was rich. He's what you call a persona au gratin with her." Sadie assembled the cards in her hand and made a neat stack. "No, Sam, we got to do it the hard way. I've got to call all these people, get them here to speak to me, make some notes on them, and find a nice woman for Harry and another Jacob for Doris."

"That should only take seven or eight years."

"So we might as well start." Sadie took her reading glasses from the pocket of her housecoat and adjusted them on her nose. She segregated the cards by sex and handed the men to Sam. "Let's first take out the ones that are the right ages for Harry and Doris, then we'll make a list to call and start with the appointments."

"And what about Brenda Fogelman."

"Don't remind me," Sadie said. "I'm still trying to figure that girl out."

Sam looked up as the doorbell rang. "I'll bet you that's our resident fruitcake," he said as he went to the door. Bryna Pernik walked into the apartment with mascara-streaked cheeks, sniffling into a handkerchief. "Sadie," she said, her voice breaking, "she has to help me . . ."

"In the kitchen," Sadie called. She rose to meet Bryna and was more than a little alarmed when the young girl fell into her arms, sobbing.

"Now, now," Sadie said as she hugged Bryna, "it can't be that bad. Sha, sha, and stop crying . . ."

"My grandmother," Bryna sobbed.

"Again with your grandmother," Sam said. His eyebrows rose to touch his hairline.

"Of course, her grandmother," Sadie said. She sat Bryna down in a chair at the table and, fetching a tissue, dabbed at the girl's cheeks. "Why is it we hurt flesh and blood worse than we do strangers?" she asked the world at large. "Calm down now, cookie, and tell me everything."

Bryna sniffled a few times, then blew her nose loudly. "We had a fight," she managed to say.

"Over the fruitcake," Sam said.

Bryna nodded, collected her breath, and swallowed hard. "I went to see her—with my last fruitcake . . ."

"The one I tasted yesterday? With too much cinnamon?"

Bryna nodded. "She tasted it and smiled in a funny way and I got so angry. Then I pleaded with her to give me the recipe and she refused. I began to yell at her . . . I said something . . ." Bryna paused, looking at the floor.

"What?" Sadie asked.

"I can't tell you," Bryna said, "not even in Hungarian."

"Oh, boy," Sam said, "it must have been terrible."

"Awful," Bryna nodded, "and very stupid of me. She got white, very mad, and she threw me out of her apartment, and told me not to come back, and she's never talking to me again as long as she lives!" And with this, Bryna began sobbing once more. "What'll I do, Sadie?" she cried, "what'll I do?"

"First calm yourself, then we'll talk. Crying doesn't help, except for exercising your eyes." Sadie busied herself, making a pot of tea, giving Bryna time to calm herself. Some little time later they sat drinking tea.

"For months now," Bryna said, "I've been trying to figure out why she won't part with her recipe. And I can't. It's a mystery. Why won't she give it to me? Why?"

"Why?" Sadie echoed. "Who can ever tell the reasons some people have in their heads and in their hearts? I had an Aunt Augusta, she should rest, threw out her husband Herman one fine day after thirty-two and a half years of marriage. Boom! Just like that. Herman came home from work and found his suitcases packed in the hallway, the lock on the door changed, and that was it, he was out in the cold. Not another day did they live together, those two, and when Herman died, seven years later, he was still asking 'Why?' The only answer Augusta ever gave the poor man was 'He knows darn well why.'"

"That's awful," Bryna said.

"Terrible. It was only years later, when Augusta began that business with kidnapping parakeets and holding them for ransom, that we figured out she had become a cuckoobird herself. But poor Herman never knew why."

"I know why," Bryna said. "Grandma hate me."

"I'm sure that's not it," Sadie said.

"Ever since we escaped from Budapest I've wanted to be able to make that fruitcake. It's the only thing Grandma makes that I can't."

"Maybe that's it," Sam said. "Maybe she figures if she parts with that recipe you won't need her any more, so she's guarding it with her life. Her one secret from you."

"Sam, if you knew her you wouldn't say that. She's so sweet, so kind . . . and I've made an enemy of her."

"A grandma can't be an enemy," Sadie said. "You'll apologize to her, she'll kiss you, and you'll be friends again. You'll see, Bryna."

"She won't give me that recipe. I know it."

Sadie looked into Bryna's tear-rimmed eyes, then took out her pen. She handed Bryna a blank index card. "Write down for me her name and address."

"You'll see her?" Bryna leaned over and kissed Sadie's cheek.

"Sometime tomorrow," Sadie said, "I'm going to get to the bottom of your Hungarian Fruitcake."

"Are you sure you have to go?" Maxine Morris was saying. She held her hands on Michael's cheeks and drew his head closer, then gently kissed his chin, the tip of his nose, and his left eyelid.

Michael groaned. "Oh, God, I wish I didn't have to."

"Then don't." She nestled close against his chest, her arms about him.

Almost automatically, Michael squeezed her to him. "Duty calls, Max. I have to be in the O.R. at six. That's only a few hours from now. I've got to get some sleep."

"Stay," she murmured, "please . . ."

"Got to go," said Michael. He kissed her hair and hugged her again. "I'm going to be fixing someone's nose with a knife in my hand, and I can't do that without sleep. So good night." He released her and walked to the closet to get his coat.

Maxine followed and watched as he put on his topcoat. "Stay ten more minutes."

"Behave yourself," Michael said.

"Why should I start now?"

Michael buttoned his topcoat. "I'm going to go downstairs, hope someone hasn't stolen my car, drive across the park, put my car in the garage, go upstairs and get into bed." He looked at her eyes. "That's what I'm going to do." He stood unmoving. "Soon I'm going to do that."

"Have you thought about moving in with me?" asked Maxine.

"Yes. Among other things."

"If you lived here, you'd be home already."

"You sound like a sign near a housing development."

"I think we ought to talk about it, Michael."

"We will, but not now." He looked at his watch. "It's almost two in the morning. Goodbye." He moved toward the door.

"I think it makes sense for us to live together," Maxine said.

"So do I. We'll have to talk about it. Soon."

She put her arms about him and rubbed the top of her head against his chin. "Your coat smells of mothballs," she said.

"Sorry."

"No, I like it." She took his hand and kissed his fingers, one by one. Then she unbuttoned the top button of his topcoat.

"Oh, God," Michael sighed, "you're impossible." He didn't stop her as she unbuttoned the rest of his coat and helped him off with it. "Thirty minutes, no more . . . who am I kidding?" he said, as Maxine began to giggle.

Thirteen

Fred Dubin was already seated at their table when Brenda Fogelman entered the chic restaurant in SoHo. He stood, appraising Brenda as she made her way to him through the dining room. She had taken some pains with her appearance, he could see. Her overalls had no patches and the flannel shirt she wore underneath if not new was at least clean. And Brenda's wild mane of bushy black hair was tied back in a pony tail, held by a red rubber band.

"What a fancy place," Brenda said, "can you afford it?" She took his hand in her sculptor's grip and squeezed.

"Easy there," Dubin said, wincing, "you don't have to break my fingers." He held her chair for her as she sat down. "I wasn't sure you'd come. It's apparently not easy to get a message to you."

"You called Hymie Farrel, right?"

"The man who owns the gallery, yes."

"And he called the doll factory on the floor below me.

Next time you want me, call them direct—Bitsey Baby Dolls—and they'll come up and call me to the phone."

"Fine." Dubin held up a hand and a waiter appeared at his shoulder. "Two Americanos, please, on the rocks." The waiter nodded and turned away.

"I don't drink."

"It's an aperitif. It's not like drinking."

Brenda shrugged. "I don't want you to waste your money, is all."

"It's not my money. I'm on an expense account. And we'll be talking business."

"Okay," Brenda said. "What's an Americano anyway?"

"Campari . . . vermouth, soda. . . . You may like it. If not, just stare at it." Dubin looked at Brenda's hands which were drumming nervously at the edge of the table. They showed signs of recent exposure to soap and water, although her fingernails were edged in black. "Have you finished that large piece you were working on? Farrel told me about it. He thinks it's very good."

"Almost finished. I still have some soldering to do. And maybe a little blowtorch work."

"Farrel said he's going to make it the centerpiece of the show. I'll have to see it sometime."

"Maybe after lunch," Brenda said. "We could walk over to my studio and you could come up and see it."

"Some other time. I have an appointment after lunch."

"Okay." There was a short silence. Brenda stared at her hands. "I've been thinking about you a lot," she said.

"For heaven's sake, why?"

Brenda shrugged. "I don't know. I just have."

"Don't get any ideas," Dubin said. "This is strictly business."

"Yeah, yeah, I know that." She smiled, nervously. "Listen, I'm more surprised than you are. I'm not terrific in the boy-girl department."

"That doesn't surprise me."

"Not that I'm a total innocent. I could tell you stories about things I've done that'd curl your hair."

The waiter placed their drinks down before them. "We'll order lunch soon," Dubin told him, "so don't disappear." He picked up his drink and held it before his eyes. "Here's to your work, and a fantastic opening."

Brenda smiled and took a cautious sip. "Hey, that's not bad."

"It grows on you."

Brenda took a healthy slug of her drink. "Nice."

"Easy girl," Dubin cautioned, "this isn't Coca-Cola. And you shouldn't gulp like that. Sip it, like me."

"Sorry." Brenda put her drink down. "Listen, Dubin," she began, "what do people call you?"

"My name is Fred Dubin," he shrugged, "take your pick."

"Funny, I keep thinking of you as Freddie. Do you mind?"

Dubin shook his head. "Whatever you like," he said. "Let's talk about the opening. I've suggested to Farrel, and he's agreed, that it be more formal, in terms of dress, than is usual down here. No jeans, overalls, things like that. And if people want to come in evening clothes, they are to be encouraged. I want the crowd to look elegant."

"Why the hell do you want that?" Brenda said. "My friends don't own evening clothes, for God's sake."

"Then let them rent." He held up a hand to still Brenda's protest. "Listen to me, now. I know precisely what I'm doing, and how I'm going to get the opening on film. It's contrast, don't you see? Your work on display, spotlighted—rough-hewn, hard-edged pieces of metal, unfinished really but full of a terrible energy and vitality, like America, maybe. And all around your work, elegant ladies and spiffy gents, the avant garde at its worst, perhaps a few recognizable jet-setters, if we're lucky. And then you, Brenda, the artist, in your usual costume. And not the way you are today, girl. I want you wearing that filthy shirt and those dirty overalls I saw you wearing last time. And your hair must be wild—not tied back so neatly."

Brenda finished her drink. "You're out of your gourd, Freddie."

"Like a fox, my dear. Trust me. I know what I'm creating."

"A Frankenstein," Brenda said. "Is that it?"

"No, a Brenda Fogelman," Dubin said smoothly. "The new artist everyone in this town is going to be talking about. A Brenda Fogelman."

"In other words, a freak."

"A freak? No, not at all. The picture I see is of a really dedicated artist—young, daring, putting all of herself into her work, holding nothing back, caring nothing for society's normal code of dress, behavior, standards. In other words, to use your phrase, the real Brenda Fogelman."

Brenda stared at the television director in the handsome suede jacket, noting the clouds that darted across his brow as he spoke, the wicked slash of his moustache, the thrust of his solid chin. And that strange feeling she had inside, that knot of tension, desire and nerve, tightened. "Holy mackerel," she said, "you're some hunk, you know that?"

Dubin laughed. "I don't think you'd better drink any more of that," he said.

The neighborhood was getting very Hungarian.

Sadie walked past the little Budapest Restaurant, just down the street from a nightclub called Czardas. A sign in a food store window declared: "We have fresh paprika." Find fresh paprika, she thought, and a Hungarian must be close by. She looked at the address Bryna had given her. Yes, Maria Pernik, Bryna's grandmother, lived only a few doors away. Over a delicatessen, in fact, which reminded Sadie of Sam's old joke: "If I had my life to live over, I'd live over a delicatessen." She wondered if Maria Pernik felt that way.

Ten minutes after Sadie knocked on the door, she and Mrs. Pernik were old friends. Mrs. Pernik had seen Sadie many times on television, and while the tea was steeping she wanted to know everything about the world of celebrities. "Merv Griffing I like," she said. "Is he okay?"

"A sweetheart."

"And Doctor Joyce Brothers?"

"A nice person," Sadie said, "and a terrific knitter besides."

Maria served the tea and sat down beside Sadie. On the table was a plate of raisin and nut twists. "I'm pinching myself," Maria said, "sitting in my own kitchen with *the* Sadie Shapiro, a real celebrity."

"What celebrity?" Sadie grinned. "I'm a plain United States person."

"Eat something," Maria insisted, "have a *ruggle*—I baked them only yesterday."

Sadie took a nut and raisin twist. "Mmm," she said, still chewing, "I'm not from the bakers, but this is something special. Now I see where Bryna gets her cooking talent. From you, Maria."

"Of course, from me."

"She's always talking about what a wonderful cook and baker you are."

Maria Pernik nodded at Sadie. She took a sip of her tea. "Now I know why Bryna send you here," she said. "It's about fighting with me . . . and fruitcake, yes?" A cloud passed over the old grandmother's face. "I wish I never made that fruitcake," she went on, "then Bryna and me would not have such trouble between us."

"Bryna says it's really a very good fruitcake."

"Not very good, *the best*."

"Then tell me, Maria," Sadie said, "why won't you give the recipe to Bryna?"

Maria Pernik drew breath sharply. "This is not your business."

"Bryna is a friend, Maria, and I'm trying to help. Why won't you give Bryna what she wants?"

"Why?" Mrs. Pernik echoed, her lips set, "why?" The tall woman with a coif of silvery braided hair arose from the table and walked to the window. She stared out, then turned to Sadie. "Very personal, this thing," she said.

"Important things always are, Maria."

"Very difficult to speak about . . ."

"Tell me, then," Sadie said gently. "You know you always feel better when you tell someone a secret."

Maria Pernik nodded, then crossed her arms over her chest. "Why I do not give Bryna the recipe is this—there is no recipe to give her."

The words fell so quietly from Maria's lips that Sadie was not sure she had heard them correctly. "No recipe?" she asked.

"Back in Hungary, many years ago, my mother teach me to make that fruitcake. And Sadie, that is the way I make it still, by memory. With only my eyes and my hands and my memory."

"A memory cake!" Sadie exclaimed. "I see now, Maria. There really is no written-down recipe to give to Bryna, is there?"

"No recipe," said Maria Pernik, "only in my head."

"Of course," Sadie said. She thought for a moment. "Then tell me, why in all these years couldn't you make the cake and write down the recipe for Bryna, or even for yourself? You know, Maria, you measure the flour and make a note, put in the eggs and make a note. And when you're finished you've got a cake and a recipe. You could do that, Maria."

"Could not," said Mrs. Pernik.

"Of course you could," Sadie said.

"No." Maria Pernik lowered her eyes and stared at the floor.

"It's so simple," Sadie said in her sunny way. "You just write down every step, you see?"

"I can not write," Maria Pernik said in a whisper. She looked at Sadie strangely, tears brimming behind her lashes.

Dear God, Sadie thought, I should have guessed. Quickly she rose and went to Maria, enfolding her in a gentle hug. In Sadie's arms, Maria Pernik let down her defenses and cried.

It took some time to calm her, but not more than ten minutes later she was sitting at the kitchen table with Sadie, sipping her tea. "Can not write, can not read," she said. "Not Hungarian, and not English. Only to sign my name—this I can do. This is my secret, Sadie, for many, many years. I keep it from everyone, and always I am so ashamed. Most important I keep my secret from my lovely Bryna, you see? What she think of me if she know, eh? Stupid old woman, Maria Pernik, can not write one word."

"Let's not talk stupid," Sadie said. "Listen, it's no crime not to be able to read and write English. If it was they would have locked up my own mother."

"So ashamed, Sadie. Terrible this feeling. And now my Bryna is angry. So what can I do? I will not tell her about . . . not writing. So I can not give her this recipe, not ever. So what can I do?"

"Oh, that?" said Sadie with an airy wave. "That I already got figured out. You're going to make the fruit-cake, Maria, and I'm going to do the writing down."

Before Maria could say a word, Sadie had everything organized. The two women went down to the street to shop for all the necessary ingredients to make the fruit-cake. And on the way back Sadie detoured them to a housewares store where she purchased a full set of measuring cups and spoons.

"I think I bought everything but a tape measure," Sadie said as they unloaded packages onto Maria's kitchen table. "Now you be the baker, and I'll be your private secretary." Sadie found her pad and pencil deep in the bottom of her knitting bag. She turned to a fresh page and wrote in her flowing hand. "I'm calling it, 'Maria Pernik's Hungarian Fruitcake.' Unless you object?"

"Beautiful," Maria beamed.

"Okey-dokey. We got a snappy title, now let's make a lovely cake. What's first?"

"Measure the flour."

"Ahah! So you really do have some way to measure."

Maria went to the cabinet above the sink and took down an old blue china bowl. She showed it to Sadie. "This chip, you see? Right here? I fill with flour up to this chip—that is the right amount for the cake." And with that, she reached for the sack of cake flour.

"Wait!" Sadie cried, "first we have to measure."

Bryna looked sheepishly at Sadie. "Of course." She took the measuring cup from the table and, under Sadie's watchful eye, carefully leveled each cup of flour with the edge of a knife before dumping it into the old, blue bowl.

"Scant four cups of cake flour," Sadie wrote on her pad when the flour was measured. "What's next?"

"Chop up brandied cherries, raisins and currants."

"And how do you measure those, Maria?"

"By handfuls."

"Fine," said Sadie, "but before you add them to the mixing bowl, let's put them into a measuring cup."

With Sadie and Maria working as a team—adding a smidgen here, subtracting a soupçon there—the "handful" ingredients were brought into measurable proportions and Sadie added them to the recipe. The liquid ingredients went smoothly, too, and in half an hour, the two women had worked their way through the butter, sugar, egg yolks, cider, tart jelly, and a secret ingredient, a full cup of yogurt.

Here Maria paused, a worried expression on her face. "Trouble now," she said. "Adding molasses."

"Why is that trouble?"

"Because . . ." Maria said. "How I do it, I pour molasses into everything until I see certain color. How you going to write down a *color*?"

"Let me think for a minute," Sadie said as she paced about the neat kitchen. Then she was nodding emphatically. "We have to do this backwards," she announced somewhat mysteriously. Taking a one-quart measuring cup, she filled it with molasses and handed it to Maria. "Now you go ahead and pour, and when you get the color you need, stop, and I'll do a little subtracting. Believe me, it's going to work."

Very slowly, Maria poured molasses into the mixing bowl, stirring all the while with a large wooden spoon. "Okay!" she exclaimed as she suddenly stopped pouring. "Color is just right."

Sadie took the large measuring cup of molasses and held it at eye level. "Don't tell anyone, but you just measured out exactly seven eighths of a cup of molasses." She wrote it down on her pad.

"Next I do pinches," said Maria. "Baking powder, salt, baking soda, cinnamon. How to do this?"

"Waxed paper," Sadie said, "that's what we need." Maria brought Sadie a roll of waxed paper from the cupboard. "Now," Sadie said, "instead of pinching those ingredients into the bowl, pinch them onto the waxed paper and I'll measure them."

"Smart lady," Maria said, smiling. She pinched, Sadie measured, and then while Maria added the ingredients to the cake, Sadie added her measurements to the recipe. "Next?"

"Nuts."

"Nuts to you, too," Sadie joked. "How much nuts?"

"I make a mound high as my hand on table, then chop."

"Make me a mound and then I'll measure."

The rest was simple for Maria's practiced hands to do and for Sadie's to record. Sadie made sure of the baking pan's size by looking underneath to read the manufacturer's imprint. The oven temperature she noted for herself, and the fact that Maria buttered and floured the pan before pouring in the batter. When the cake was in the oven the two women shared a second pot of tea.

"Baking very slow and low oven for good fruitcake," Maria said. "Must not be dry."

"Can you tell me how long it should bake?" Sadie asked.

"Of course," Maria smiled, "three hours about. Time I can read."

"Do you put a toothpick in the center to test it?"

"No toothpick. When you push gentle with finger, cake comes back up again. Easy to tell."

"For you I'm sure it is," Sadie said. She made a last note, then handed the recipe to Maria. "Now you got a cake in the oven, and a recipe in your hand for Bryna."

The warmth reflected on Maria's face almost matched that of the oven. "Sweet Sadie," she said, "you are most wonderful in America. How I ever thank you enough?"

"That's easy." Sadie began gathering her things. "By making up with Bryna again."

"Yes. I do that. And give her recipe, of course."

"That's the answer," Sadie said. Maria embraced her, and walked Sadie to the door. The white-haired grandmother had one more request and she was nervous as she spoke. "My secret—you know? Please, you do not tell Bryna I can not write so she think I am stupid."

"Not in a million years," Sadie said. She smiled. "And besides, who says you have to tell a granddaughter *everything?*"

Fourteen

"I only have five minutes." Fred Dubin was grumbling as he climbed the stairs behind Brenda. "Just time for a quick look at your new sculpture and then I'm off."

"Right, right," Brenda called back as she scampered quickly up the last flight. She turned on the landing and shot a smile back at Dubin. "Come on, slowpoke."

"I'm coming." Dubin looked up at the girl waiting for him. "You must be half mountain goat. You're not even winded."

"I'm not." Brenda extended a hand to Dubin as he slowly climbed the last half-flight of stairs. "I know it's hard on you older people," she mocked. "Shall I help you up?"

"Older people my clavicle. Behave yourself, squirt, before I take you over my knee."

"Promises, promises," Brenda grinned. She opened the metal door and waited for Dubin.

The loft looked very different, Dubin saw as he entered Brenda's studio. The girl had made an effort to clean up the place. The floor was clear of litter now and appeared to have been painted. The large, grimy windows had been cleaned. Where Brenda's soiled, uncovered mattress used to be there was now a bright blue air mattress with a neatly rolled sleeping bag at its foot. New, too, were the small round white table and matching director's chairs arranged in a conversational grouping. The place looked livable, Dubin thought, not *House & Garden* by any means, but suitable perhaps for a monk or an artist.

"What do you think?" Brenda asked. "Not so slobby any more, huh?"

"Not bad." Dubin nodded. "A start, anyway."

"Not bad?" Brenda echoed, "I spent over a hundred bucks fixing this place and that's all you can say?"

"It's nice," Dugan said, "neat, really, and it suits you, Brenda."

"That's better." She took Dubin's hand and led him to the table and chairs. "I wanted you to be the first to sit in my chairs. And this one is just for you." She turned the canvas chair and showed Dubin the back of it. On the upper backrest the word "Freddie" had been stenciled in bright blue. "Your own personal chair," she grinned. "Sit down."

Dubin hesitated, looking at the young artist. This is silly, he started to say and then stopped himself. Brenda looked so open, so vulnerable, so expectant of something he could not give her. And yet, hardened to life and to women as he was, he did not want to hurt this girl. She was so incredibly young and naive, so direct and unsophisticated. And yes, her gesture of creating his own chair did touch something inside him, no matter how slightly. He sat down in the chair and smiled at her.

116

"That's better," she said in a bubbly voice. "My own director in his own director's chair."

"It was very sweet of you to do this."

"Sweet, hell. I'm nuts about you, Freddie, as you can probably tell by now. I want to do more for you than this."

"Brenda . . ."

"What do I have to do, draw you a picture?"

"Brenda, stop. We're friends now, which is more than I could say a few weeks ago. Let's be very careful, please, not to go beyond that."

"That's no fun," Brenda said, only half seriously. "Are you seeing someone? Is that it?"

"That's none—" Dubin caught himself before he said more. "Yes," he lied, "I am . . . For a long time now. I'm sorry . . ."

Brenda nodded, her lips set. "Okay, so I've got competition. I'll handle it. Probably some old broad, huh?"

"Ancient. Practically a relic."

"I figured," Brenda said. "I'm going to be twenty-six in a couple of months. How old are you?"

"Thirty-nine," Dubin said, adding two years to his age.

"That's not too old for me. When you're fifty I'll be thirty-eight, that's not too bad."

Dubin laughed at the intently serious expression on her face.

"You're incredible," he said. "Is there anything I can say to turn you off?"

"I doubt it. I'm on your trail, Freddie, and I don't like to lose." She began moving toward him. Dubin stood up and, before he could take any action to fend her off, found himself encircled by her arms. She squeezed him for just a moment. "You *are* a hunk," she said. For one of the few times in his life, Dubin had no words. He stood and let her hug him, looking across the wide loft at the vivid metal sculptures across the room, feeling the strength in Brenda's young arms. "Aren't you even going to kiss me?" she asked.

With what might have been a fatherly feeling, Dubin took Brenda's face in his hands and held it. Then he leaned down and kissed her, on the forehead. When she tried to cling to him again he gently pried her away from her grasp. "Easy now," he said. "I do have to get moving." Calmly, playing down what had transpired between them, he walked to the door.

"Freddie," Brenda called after him, "that's not what I call a kiss."

"I'll call you." A puzzled look came onto his face. "Bidey Baby Dolls, right?"

"Bitsey Baby Dolls."

"Right." He stared at her for a moment. "Be good now and finish that big piece for your show."

"I will," she said. "And Freddie, you can come up and put your tush in that chair anytime you like."

But Dubin was already disappearing from her doorway. Brenda walked to the hallway and listened to his tread on the stairs. She waited until she could hear no more, then walked back into her studio. A strikeout, she thought, a big fat zero. I'm about as sexy as a tree. "Dammit!" she cried out. Taking up her ball peen hammer, she approached her massive sculpture, whacking it five, six times in succession. "Dammit!" she cried again, and this time there were tears in her eyes. Twenty-six years she'd spent keeping men at arm's length, being her own woman and going her own way. Now there was one man she wanted, permanently, and she didn't know how to get him.

"KONG!" The sound reverberated through the studio as she struck the hollow metal sculpture. Back in high school, when all the girls began to pluck and tweeze their eyebrows, she had wanted to make hers grow bushier. Perhaps those stupid girls were right, after all.

"KONG!" Those endless, running arguments with her mother over clothing, the forced shopping trips she was dragged along on, the feminine clothes she had refused to wear all these years. Fashion! Yuch, she hated the word and, what's more, did not know what it was about. Could it be possible that her mother was right?

"KONG!" She'd thrown herself at Freddie and he'd caught her gently and thrown her back like a fish too small to keep. There had to be other ways to make him want her, other approaches beyond merely flinging herself into his arms. But who knew about such things? Who had the wisdom and the experience to tell her what to do? Who in this whole wide world could help her make Freddie want her in return? Who?

"KONG!"

"So that was the secret of the Hungarian Fruitcake," Sam was saying. "Now I understand why Mrs. Pernik was so upset."

Sadie was sitting in the yellow club chair, her slippered feet resting on an ottoman. It had been a long day. "It's a secret, Sam," she said, "you mustn't tell it to a single soul, or a married one either."

"My lips are sealed."

"Good," Sadie said. "Loose lips not only sink ships, they're terrible for dentures besides. Mr. Pernik will work it out with Bryna in her own way and time, and we'll both be make-believe surprised when Bryna comes marching in here with the real fruitcake."

Sam took a pull on his cigar. He reached over to the cocktail table and pulled an ashtray near, then carefully flicked an inch of white ash off the end of his cigar. "You know something?" he said. "I really don't like fruitcake, even a good one."

"Neither do I," Sadie grinned, "but we're both going to tell Bryna it's delicious when she comes running in here."

"Of course," Sam nodded as the doorbell rang. "That could be a fruitcake call," he said as he went to the door.

Harry Wald was standing in the hallway. There was a gray cast to his face and he looked grim and worried. "Can I come in?" he asked. "Is Sadie here?"

Sam led the fruit man to the living room, looking him over as he walked to Sadie and shook her hand. Wald looked somewhat neater than the last time Sam had seen him. The awful stained and ripped zipper jacket was gone, replaced by an obviously new windbreaker in olive drab. Sam could tell the jacket was new because the manufacturer's ticket was still stapled to the bottom of the side pocket.

"I'm sorry to come crashing in on you like this," Wald said. "I've got to talk to you, Sadie."

"Of course. Take off your jacket, sit down."

Wald unzipped himself and handed the jacket to Sam. "Your husband smartened me up," he said to Sadie. "You see, Sam, I got all new clothes."

"I see." Sam shielded his hand from Wald with the jacket and worked the little stapled ticket free.

"A new jacket, new sweatshirt, new blue jeans, and new work boots. Do I still look like a panhandler to you?"

"No," Sam said, "now you look like a construction worker." Wald looked quizzically at Sam. "Never mind, Harry, we'll talk about that later. I'm sure you didn't come here for sartorial advice."

"No," Wald said, "I'm here because I'm going out of

my mind. Sadie, you've got to help me. I can't eat, I can't sleep, thinking about her. All day long when I walk around it's like there's a bell ringing in my mind, and that bell is ringing, 'Man-del-*Baum*, Man-del-*Baum*, Man-del-*Baum*!' You've got to make Doris give me one more chance!" In his passion, Wald's voice had risen an octave, and there was a wild look in his eyes.

"Take it easy, Mr. Wald," Sadie cautioned. "You get all excited like that your heart can decide to go take a walk and then where will you be? I'll make us all a nice cup of tea, you'll calm yourself, and then we'll talk."

Wald sat silently on the couch, staring across the room, as Sadie busied herself in the kitchen. Watching him, looking so forlorn and lost, Sam felt a sympathy for the fruit tycoon. Once, not so long ago, he had been in the same situation. For two years he had seen Sadie every day, coming to know and love her as time went by. And then, when he had proposed Sadie move in with him without benefit of marriage, she had gone away. It was then, bereft and alone, that he realized he would make any sacrifice, change any principle he held, to have her back and close to him again. Of such feelings are marriages made. But poor Harry Wald, he had not even gone through a courtship with the icy Doris Mandelbaum, probably he had not even held her hand. And yet, the strong grip of love and need held him in its grasp.

"Tea is made," Sadie announced from the kitchen doorway.

They seated themselves around the kitchen table and Sadie poured. A few moments later, Wald was pouring out his heart. "Honest and true now, Sadie, you got me figured for a no-goodnik as far as Doris is concerned. Isn't that so?"

Sadie measured her words. "Not completely true, no. You're a nice, sweet man. I, personally, like you. So does

Sam." She raised her eyebrows in an expressive way. "The problem is Doris Mandelbaum would kill me if I sent you to see her again, that's all."

"And with me, it's Doris or nobody!"

Sadie sighed, struck once again by the absolute impossibility of predicting how love could bloom in the unlikeliest places, and to the unlikeliest people. "Invest in a fever," she said, "and your profit is a disease. I understand, Mr. Wald, but Doris is being a real stubborn Susie."

"Speak to her again," Wald said. "Please."

"I did speak to her again," Sadie said, remembering the conversation with a silent shudder. "The answer was no."

Wald's face clenched and unclenched. He took a sip of his tea without tasting it. "I mean *again* again."

"All right," Sadie said. There was a short silence before she spoke again. "You know, Mr. Wald, I looked at the cards I got from Sarah Barish the other day. And the mystery to me is how Sarah ever sent you to Doris in the first place. I mean, from what she wrote on your card, Doris would not be the right woman for you."

"That card was written a long time ago," he said. "I've changed a lot since then."

Sadie got up from the table and fetched the matchmaker's old tea tin from the top of the refrigerator. She took out Harry Wald's card. "Read it," she said as she handed it to him. Then, as Wald scanned the card she recited it aloud, for she knew it by heart. "It says you're a clean, plain-looking man who dresses bad."

"Not so bad any more," Wald put in. "I'm buying new clothes."

"We'll talk about that later, Harry," Sam said.

Sadie cleared her throat. "It also says you want a warm, quiet woman and she should be a good cook. A homebody, you asked for." Sadie smiled at the fruit man. "That doesn't sound anything at all like Doris Mandelbaum, does it?"

Harry Wald nodded, looking silently at Sadie. His fingers danced nervously on the table. In the silence, Sadie sat down in her chair once again.

Wald sighed. "You know what that card is," he began. "That is a description of my Emily. That's the way she was. Quiet, a woman who was happy to cook and clean and keep a nice home. And when I went to the Matchmaker that's what I told her I was looking for—another Emily. But, you know, you get a little older, time passes, and maybe you learn a little. There can never be another Emily. I understand that now." Wald's voice tightened and he coughed to conceal it. He took a sip of tea. To Sadie, it was clear the man was on the verge of tears.

"Tell you what," she said brightly, "we'll start again. I'll make a brand-new card for you, how's that? One of my own." Before Wald could reply she had risen and left the room. She went to her desk in the corner of the living room and brought back a pen and a blank index card. "Okay," she announced, forcing the gaiety into her voice, "ipsy-pipsy and okey-dokey, we'll make a brand new card for you. And with luck, you'll find a brand-new wife." She sat down at the table, uncapped her felt-tip pen, and began. "Give me your whole name, Harry."

"Herschel Benjamin Wald, that's what it says on my birth certificate. But everyone calls me Harry. A few people, old friends, call me Ben."

Sadie wrote Wald's whole name on the card. "I always loved the name Benjamin," she smiled. "Age?"

"Fifty-eight. And my address and phone number are the same."

Sadie wrote the information on the card in her small,

neat hand. "Okay, now we get to the hard part, all about you." She gazed at him critically. "How would you describe yourself?"

Wald thought for a moment. "Handsome?" he asked, smiling. "Some people say I look like Charlton Heston."

"Only your nose," Sadie said. "I'd say you were a very pleasant-looking man."

"Pleasant?" Wald's eyebrows rose and fell. "Who wants to be described as 'pleasant'? Couldn't you stretch it a little to good-looking?"

Sam laughed at the look on Wald's face. "I think he's *adorable*, myself."

Sadie grinned at Wald. "Okay, *attractive*." She wrote the word on Wald's new card. "I won't write dresses bad because you're taking care of that, right?"

"*I'm* taking care of that," Sam announced.

"What else should I put down for you?" Sadie asked.

"How about *rich*?" Sam said.

Wald winced at the word. "No, no, not rich," he protested.

Sam looked coolly at Wald. "Were you fooling, Harry, or what? Forty-eight fruit stores, a wholesale fruit business, plus you own land and fruit groves in Florida and Arizona? Why not rich?"

Wald pursed his lips, hunched his shoulders. He looked as if he had just tasted a lemon. "I hate that word, that's all. I mean, if you're rich you don't go around advertising it. I would say I'm . . . comfortable."

"Fruit groves and land in two states is more than comfortable," Sam insisted.

"And also in Texas and Oregon, I forgot to mention that," Wald said.

"I'm impressed," Sadie said. "Rich or poor, at least you've got money. But why didn't you tell the Matchmaker all this?"

Wald shrugged. "Does Macy's tell Gimbels?"

"I'm putting down 'wealthy' on your card, Mr. Wald, and I promise I won't go around advertising it, okay?" Wald began to protest, then decided against it. He nodded his head sheepishly. "Okay, now tell me more about yourself. I want information."

"College graduate," Wald said. "Member of the Chamber of Commerce in five states, Kiwanis, a few other organizations. I'm a sponsor of the Brooklyn Academy of Music, the Brooklyn Museum . . ."

"An intellectual!" Sadie said warmly. "That's very good!"

"Well," Wald shrugged, "they ask for money and I send them some. Brooklyn's my home town after all. What else? I belong to the Book-of-the-Month Club *and* the Literary Guild . . ."

"A reader, terrific."

" . . . subscriber to *Time, The Wall Street Journal,* and the *Wholesale Fruiterer.* I like to see plays, listen to music, and I'm crazy about sports."

"Unfortunately, Doris Mandelbaum hates sports," Sadie said. "How about opera? Doris loves opera."

"Then I love opera," Wald said. "Listen, I can learn . . ."

Sadie was writing note after note, finally turning the card over to write on the back of it. Herschel Benjamin Wald was growing in her estimation, minute by minute. If only he would let himself grow as well. The man appeared to be . . . well, cheap, to put it bluntly. He was, if not rich, at least comfortable. And yet he had fumbled away his one date with Doris Mandelbaum. An old suit, an old car, and Doris had pegged Harry as an ordinary shnook. As Sadie herself had, too, until she had learned better. Harry Wald had hidden his light under a basket, an old fruit basket at that.

"Next, Mr. Wald," Sadie said, "I got to ask you the sixty-four dollar question. The kind of woman you're looking for."

Wald grinned. "Put down Doris Mandelbaum."

"This I know already," Sadie said. "But you know, a piano has eighty-eight keys, you can't keep playing on one all the time. It's possible I can find another nice woman for you."

"Not interested," Wald said. "Doris or nothing."

Sadie looked over at Sam, who coughed and stubbed out his cigar in the ashtray. He shrugged at her. The man was smitten and would not be budged. Right now other women did not exist for Harry Wald. "I'll try," Sadie said at last. "She'll throw me out, lock, smock, and blankets, but I'll go back to see her again."

Wald reached across the table and patted Sadie's hand. "Thank you," he said, "thank you very much. I'm going to go home and say a prayer that she'll let me have one more chance."

The telephone rang and Sadie glanced at the kitchen clock. It was late for a telephone call, at least in her experience. Calls at this hour of the night usually meant bad news. She got up and went to the wall phone near the window.

"Stay a minute before you go," Sam told Wald. He looked at Sadie. "Who's on the phone?"

Sadie had her hand over the mouthpiece, listening to the caller, shaking her head from side to side.

Sam walked Harry Wald into the living room. "Listen to me," he told the rich/wealthy/comfortable fruit merchant, "I'm going to talk to you like a Dutch uncle. You're a well-off guy, Harry, but you throw money around like glue. Now I'm telling you that if you're going to stand a chance with your Doris, or anyone else for that matter, you've got to smarten up. It's time to open

126

up your wallet, kiddo, and let some of those moths fly out. You hear what I'm saying?"

Wald nodded, not looking very happy. "Years of habit, Sam. I am very cautious with money, you're right. I guess I'll have to learn how to spend it."

"Exactly. Not throw it around, but spend it wisely. Look like a *mensh*, for heaven's sake. I know postal clerks who dress better than you."

"I bought a suit," Wald said. "Blue, formal, nice suit."

"Where?" Wald mentioned a popular, mid-priced men's clothing chain. "Forget it," Sam snapped. "I see I'll have to take you in hand, personally. What are you doing tomorrow?"

"Working?"

"Wrong. You're meeting me and I'm taking you shopping. You got credit cards? Good, bring 'em along. And your checkbook. And don't look so upset, you'll be another Valentino when I'm through with you. One more thing—you know a better woman than Doris to be spending money for?" He shook Wald's hand and escorted him to the door. "Call me tomorrow morning, ten o'clock, okay?" Sam grinned at Harry Wald. "And cheer up, Harry, it's just possible that when you start spending you might find you like it."

Sam closed the door behind Wald. He flipped the turn-lock, then slid the bolt lock into place. He walked back to the kitchen. Sadie was sitting on the step stool, looking dazed, her telephone call concluded. "You'll never believe who called," she said.

"Who called?"

"Brenda Fogelman."

"I don't believe it. What did she say?"

"*Help!*"

Fifteen

The sun came peeping up over the RCA Building in mid-town, took one look at the sleeping city and immediately ducked behind a large gray cloud. Down in Central Park a small host of runners and joggers circled the reservoir, even at this early morning hour. Not cold and no wind, Sadie thought to herself. She turned from the window and went back into the bedroom, being careful to tread lightly. On the big double bed, under the hand-knitted comforter, Sam snored. Sadie selected one of her light-weight jogging suits from the closet, picked up her sneakers and socks, and finished dressing in the bath-room.

The air was light and refreshing as she crossed the roadway in front of her apartment building and entered the park. A group of young runners pounded by on the main roadway, waving to her, and one smiling youth called to her by name. Sadie waved and watched them disappear, wondering at the stamina and strength it took to move so fast. Youth, she thought, so brim-full of energy they can throw it away in all directions. She started jogging across the long grassy meadow, feeling the dampness of the dew under her tread. Settling into an easy, relaxed rhythm she waved her arms about as she moved to get the blood started. Let the young ones run a mile a minute, she had her own way. At her age you couldn't afford to strain the body. Slow and easy she jogged, one choppy step after another, feeling her muscles relax and tense as they moved her along, her breath shortening as the exertion built and the clarity coming into her head, as always.

People were in her head this morning, and the twisted relationships they created for themselves. Love, love, love . . . it made the world go round and drove normal people crazy. Somewhere over on Park Avenue, Doris Mandelbaum was sleeping, probably still reaching out in dreams to touch the Jacob who was no longer there. How could she show Doris that each love is different, and never twice the same, and the only place she would find her Jacob again was in heaven when she joined him there?

Doris was a woman of intelligence and breeding, and yet a simple man like Harry Wald had already learned the lesson she refused to acknowledge. Go figure that one out. And figure, while you're at it, a fruit man from Brooklyn who has one ridiculous date with the Park Avenue lady and then goes bananas over her, so much so that he will not even consider dating another woman. And that was Harry Wald's craziness, brought on by love, of course, which many times is a fatal disease.

So how was she going to make Doris Mandelbaum date Harry again? How? Well, she would go see Doris and lay her cards on the table. Maybe only one card,

Harry Wald's. And what would happen? Doris would throw her out.

Another thought intruded, so dark and worrisome she tried to push it away. Okay, let's say by some miracle Doris agrees to date Harry again. And she only confirms what she thought in the first place—Harry Wald is not for her. What then, Mrs. Matchmaker? *Gevald*, that's what, a heartache on both sides, and probably Doris and Harry would not only not speak to each other again, they'd probably not want to see me again, either.

All right, already, don't think about crossing that bridge till you come to it or you'll surely fall in the water and drown. She would see Doris and do her best. The rest was in the hands of a power higher than hers.

Out of breath now, Sadie walked, ignoring the little stitch in her side that ached with every pulse. Brenda Fogelman and Fred Dubin—talk about an odd couple. They were like oil and vinegar, those two, not mixing at all. Brenda Fogelman was crazy, but Sadie knew that when she met her the first time. How could Brenda hope to capture as stylish and assured a gentleman as Fred Dubin? How did she fall in love with him in the first place? Brenda and Dubin? He was ten years older than Brenda, at least. And he lived on a whole other planet. Brenda was the wild woman of lower Broadway, a dirty body with a dirty mouth to match. Not that Dubin couldn't use language when he wanted to, until she had convinced him not to use it when she was around. Never in a million years would a Dubin fall in love with a Brenda. Could she help the girl? Should she encourage her, or try to talk her out of it? And maybe find someone more suitable for Brenda?

Suitable for Brenda . . . Sadie smiled to herself, thinking of an ad in the newspapers. "Wanted, young man to marry a young girl who wears dirty clothes, never takes a bath, hammers and welds metal all day long, sleeps on the floor and swears like a longshoreman. Only madmen need apply."

Ay-yi-yi, Sarah Barish, you passed along a few beauties to me.

Feeling her breath come back, Sadie began to jog again. The sun came out from behind a cloud and sparkled on the wet grass. There was hope, of course, always hope as long as you kept breathing and could put one foot in front of the next one. Love was a mystery, coming and going like the sun, brightening your days when you found it, and turning day into night when it went away. But hope was cheap, thank God even poor people could afford it, and it was something to hang onto until love came along again.

Brenda and Dubin, Harry and Doris, Bryna and her grandmother, Maxine and Michael. Love to everybody, she thought, to come quick and strong and last forever. She could not wish for better than that.

Feeling light and buoyant, she rounded the pathway and jogged for home.

Upstairs, her breath back fully, Sadie stepped off the elevator. In front of her apartment door, stretched out on her back on the carpeted floor and fast asleep, lay Brenda Fogelman.

Kneeling down, Sadie touched the young artist's shoulder and nudged. Brenda's eyes opened wide. "Hello," she said, sitting up.

"And hello to you. Do you always sleep on the floor in hallways, or what?"

Brenda got to her feet. "You said to see you in the morning. It's morning."

Sadie nodded, taken aback once again by Brenda's disregard for the rules of ordinary behavior. She eyed her critically as she fished in her sweat suit pocket for the door key. Overalls with grease stains on the knee, washed-out flannel shirt, scuffed work boots complete with paint spots—the height of fashion if you were a day laborer. No makeup on that gorgeous young face, eyebrows as thick as John L. Lewis's and with a temper to match. A Brenda Fogelman and a half, as usual. "Come in and I'll make breakfast, but we'll have to be quiet because my Sam is still asleep."

She spirited Brenda into the kitchen and let her watch the water come to the boil while she slipped quietly through the bedroom and into the shower. Dressed in her favorite housecoat and mules, she returned to the kitchen. Brenda was sitting at the table, eating from a plastic container. "This is terrific," Brenda said, "what is it?"

"Last night's leftover lamb stew."

"I love it."

"I'm very glad," Sadie said. She went to the refrigerator and took out the cottage cheese. From the cupboard she took her saltines. "You could put it on a plate," she said to Brenda, "couldn't hurt."

"Nah," Brenda said, her mouth full of food, "it's okay."

Sadie's appetite, built by the jogging, was rapidly disappearing.

"Even in China they know enough to eat off plates," Sadie said. She took the plastic container from Brenda and portioned the remainder of the cold lamb stew onto a dinner plate. "Let me heat it up."

But Brenda took the plate from her and continued eating.

"I'm glad you at least learned how to use a fork," Sadie said. She spooned a dab of cottage cheese onto a saltine and chewed it slowly, watching Brenda eat. Lamb stew for breakfast, sleeping on the floor, fingernails that had never seen file or clipper, let alone a coat of polish. And this wild child had the misfortune to have set her cap for the stylish Fred Dubin. What could she possibly do for this misguided, mistaken, and completely *meshuggeneh* creature, short of throwing the old Brenda away and ordering a new one from Sears, Roebuck?

Sadie's appetite vanished completely. "All right," she sighed, "tell me more about you and Fred Dubin."

"I'm looney about him," Brenda said.

"That's the easy part," Sadie said. "And him?"

"What about him?"

"Is he in love with you? Did he say anything? Did he give you a sign?" Not only a wild child, Sadie thought, but a ninny when it came to men. She didn't need help, she needed a miracle.

"It's strictly business with Dubin," Brenda said. "He likes my work, and I think, in some way, he likes me, too. Yesterday when we were saying goodbye, he kissed me. Like a father, Sadie, that's how he kissed me. On the forehead." Brenda's dark eyes were sad.

"All right," Sadie said, "it's a start. You'd be surprised sometimes how love can start from the tiniest beginnings. I had a friend once, hit this man with her pocketbook right in the subway because she thought he was getting fresh with her, and one thing led to another, and from that smack she gave him they were married and had three lovely children. You never can tell, Brenda. A kiss on the forehead can be the beginning."

"I don't have patience, Sadie," Brenda said. "I can't wait, and I don't know how to play those flirting games, anyway. I've been throwing myself at Dubin and he isn't interested."

"Your first mistake, Brenda. You don't throw yourself until you're sure there's someone there who wants to catch you."

"I can't help myself," the young artist protested. "I see

133

him and it's like a light switches on inside me. I want to grab him, kiss him . . . I want to rip his clothes off and—"

"Hold it!" Sadie said, "and don't talk ripping and stripping. Before you get to s-e-x you've got to go through l-o-v-e, and also getting married is a definite plus."

It was Brenda's turn to be shocked. She looked at Sadie, a grin on her face. "You don't really believe that, do you?"

"Me and millions of others, cookie, no matter what you see in the movies today, with people taking their clothes off every other second. My mother used to say, 'not until the ring is on the finger,' and I still believe it today. And if ripping clothes off and jumping into bed is all you're interested in, you've come to the wrong lady. I'm certainly not going to help you do *that*, and goodbye, Brenda Fogelman." Sadie crossed her arms over her chest and looked away.

There was a long silence in the kitchen. Brenda stared at Sadie, who steadfastly refused to return her gaze. "I'm sorry," Brenda said at last.

"You should be," Sadie said. "A matchmaker makes matches, and the people usually get married. If you just want to fool around, do that on your own time. Do we understand each other, sweetie?"

Brenda nodded. "I just want to be with him," she said. "And I need your help."

"Right," Sadie said, feeling better for the first time since she'd found Brenda on her doorstep. "So stand up and turn around, I want to take a look at your figure." Brenda, wholly chastened, walked to the refrigerator and back again. "Not bad, Brenda, in fact, very good."

"I'm not wearing a bra, Sadie."

"That much is obvious, maybe a little too obvious if you take my meaning, because I'm very glad you're wearing a heavy flannel shirt and overalls on top." Sadie got up from the table and took a small tour around Brenda Fogelman. She looked at her eyes and her hair and her skin, squinting slightly as she imagined the girl with makeup, a haircut, in clothes that didn't come from the Salvation Army. "A definite beauty," she said, pinching Brenda's cheek, "and any man in his right mind would be crazy about you if you fixed yourself up a little. Are you willing to make a few changes?"

"What kind of changes?" Brenda asked cautiously.

"Improvements only, a touch here, a smidgeon there . . ."

"Will it help?"

"Couldn't hurt," Sadie started to say, only to have Brenda say it for her. The two women laughed and Sadie took Brenda's hand in a friendly squeeze. "You sound like my Aunt Leah," Brenda grinned.

"That's good."

"I *hate* my Aunt Leah, but you're okay."

Sadie nodded, her mind already working on the transformation of Brenda Fogelman. "When do you see Fred Dubin again? Do you have a date?"

Brenda shrugged. "In a couple of weeks, I suppose. When my show opens at Farrel's Gallery."

"Your opening, of course!" Sadie said. "This I know about already, from Maxine Morris. Sam and I are invited, so we'll be there. And Mr. Dubin is making a whole television show out of it, right?"

Sadie's eyes grew brighter. "But that's wonderful, Brenda! You see, he must think highly of you, to make such a production."

"My work, yes," Brenda said, "me . . ." She opened her palms and shrugged.

"Don't lose heart. It's going to be a very exciting evening, you'll be together, who knows what can happen? And you'll be all dressed up for once—"

"I'll be dressed like this," Brenda said to Sadie's uncomprehending look. "It's Freddie's idea."

"Like this?" Sadie's mouth flew open. "He wants you to look like . . . like a *himpie* . . . when everyone else is going to be dressed up beautiful? For heaven's sake, why?"

Brenda shrugged her muscular shoulders. "He has a plan in mind, Sadie . . . to make me stand out from the crowd."

"You'll stand out all right, like limburger cheese in a crowded bus."

"He wants the whole focus to be on my work, not me."

Sadie shook her head from side to side. "One thing I'm beginning to see, Brenda," she said. "Maybe you and Mister Dubin belong together . . . *because he can be as crazy as you are.*"

They came up Madison Avenue, Sam striding briskly in the morning sunshine and Harry Wald *shlepping* two paces behind. The shopping tour was in full swing and the fruit man was cranky. "How many more stores are we going to shop in?" he asked as they paused for a traffic light at the corner of Forty-eighth Street. "My feet are killing me, Sam."

"Only six or seven more. Don't worry, the next one's a shoe store, they'll take care of your feet."

"Shoes I got," Wald complained, "plenty of shoes."

"How many pairs?"

Wald thought for a moment. "These I'm wearing, plus a pair of black wingtips and a pair of brown loafers."

Sam shook his head. "The ones you're wearing we leave in the store, let the salesman throw them away. On the next corner is an English shoe store. They make a half-boot that can't be beat. One pair of brown and one pair of black, we'll buy you, then later we'll walk over to Bally and get serious."

Wald blanched. "How many pairs of shoes do I need, for God's sake?"

"Enough," Sam said. The light changed in their favor and the two men stepped off the curb, only to pull back as a hard-charging yellow taxi scooted across the avenue. The shopping trip was going well, Sam reflected, but he had to keep pushing Harry all the way. For a rich man, he hated to part with a buck, which was maybe how he got rich in the first place. At Brooks Brothers he had been fitted for three conservative suits in Brooks' classic, natural shoulder model. "They'll never go out of style," Sam had explained patiently, "for business, for a semi-formal social occasion, and they'll wear like iron." At Paul Stuart's they had shopped for sports clothes, plus some shirts, ties, and two sweaters Sam insisted Wald buy. "A fine blue blazer and gray slacks is almost like a uniform," he'd advised, "you got to have it." There had also been a pure camel's-hair blazer and chocolate slacks combination that made Wald look ten years younger, and Sam had persuaded the fruit man to buy them as well.

It was fun for Sam, passing on the expertise he had acquired over a lifetime. Years ago his Uncle Morris the Jeweler had taken him in hand. "Dress successful and you'll be successful," Morris had counseled. "Buy good and buy enough," he'd said, teaching young Sam how to rotate the wearing of his clothing, and when and how to add to his wardrobe. "Clothes make the man," Uncle Morris had said sagely, adding with a twinkle in his eye, "at least until we all start running around naked."

Sam and Harry came out of the shoe store. "Such prices," Harry said, wagging his head.

"Good doesn't come cheap." Sam inspected the shiny black half-boot Wald was wearing. "How do they feel?"

"Soft as butter. It's funny, I never wore a boot before. I didn't think they'd feel so good."

"You won't want to take them off," Sam said. He began leading Wald down East Forty-ninth Street.

"Where to next?" Wald asked. The boots felt so light on his feet he skipped for a couple of steps. Looking at his reflection in a store window, he smiled back at himself.

"Up the street to Saks' men's department, for a raincoat and a topcoat. And that *shmatte* raincoat you're wearing with the zip-in lining you zipped out we'll give to the Goodwill."

For the first time that morning, Harry Wald did not complain.

Two hours later, and several blocks further east, Maxine Morris and Michael Newman were finishing lunch at Le Perigord. Michael's thoughts were as black as the espresso before him. "This is silly," he said as he stirred a scant teaspoon of sugar into the coffee. "We're arguing over trivialities."

Maxine lit a cigarette and said nothing. The feeling she'd had for several weeks now was being confirmed. It wasn't going to work out between them, as she'd known from the first.

"Your apartment is just too inconvenient, Max. That's all. I love you and I want to be with you, can't you see that?"

"So why don't you move in with me?" Maxine said.

Michael sighed. He took a sip of the espresso. "I want to marry you, dammit, but you won't have that. Okay, so we agree to move in together and see how it goes, even though I think it's wrong. But you won't budge an inch."

"Why does it have to be your apartment?" Maxine said. "You're the one who's being stubborn."

"Because it'll be easier for *you* to move, for one thing," Michael said. "And my apartment is larger, anyway."

"Your apartment is out of the question," Maxine said. "I hate the East Side, it's so . . . *chi-chi*. Real people don't live on the East Side."

"What am I, a ghost?" Michael smiled. "Come on, babe, don't be so obstinate."

Maxine stirred sugar into her coffee, saying nothing as she watched the black liquid swirl about in her cup. She took another puff of her cigarette. Her mother had been right, as usual. A doctor was a kind of prince. Marry one and you'll do everything his way. Even this doctor, who sat smiling across the table at her, the one who could take her in his arms and make time stop. "I'm not being obstinate," she said. "My apartment is very convenient for me, which is why I live there. I can walk to my office in six minutes, and the studio we sometimes use is practically around the corner. I don't want to be across the park at your place, where I'll have to depend on cabs every day, or some stupid bus that never comes when it's raining or snowing."

"And I have an unbreakable lease and you don't," Michael said evenly, "you forgot to mention that. But putting money aside, and I'm sure my landlord won't, how about all the other things I mentioned?" He began ticking them off on his fingers. "The hospital is only a block away, my private office is around the corner, okay? The telephones—I have a tie-line to the hospital and another one to my office. I have two phones hooked into my answering service and an unlisted one for special emergencies. You know what kind of mess it would be to change all those numbers?"

"I'm sure you could keep the same phone numbers," Maxine said, "even on the West Side."

"Don't bet on it," Michael said grimly.

"I have a grocery, a butcher, and a liquor store who all know me and deliver," Max said. "That's more important than you think, Michael. Plus a great Chinese restaurant, a deli, and a pizza parlor who can send up anything I want within the hour."

"I have the same things on the East Side," Michael said. "Contrary to what you think, Max, we do sometimes eat pizza east of Fifth Avenue."

"My place is closer to your horse," Maxine said. "How about that?"

Michael nodded, conceding the point. "True, but I've gotten used to jogging across the park before taking Silver out. I don't mind it. In fact, I like it."

"A creature of habit, aren't you?" Maxine said with a sly grin. She stubbed out her cigarette in the ashtray. A waiter materialized at once and substituted a fresh ashtray in its place. Maxine checked her wristwatch, then finished her coffee in a long swallow. "I have a meeting in half an hour, on the *West Side*," she added pointedly. "I have to go."

"Wait a few minutes. We should finish this. It's important."

"So is my meeting." Maxine put her cigarettes and lighter into her handbag and snapped it closed, then sat back in her chair. Michael's face was a picture of misery, so much so that she had to reach out and clasp his hand. "Think about moving into my place," she said. "It has one great feature your apartment doesn't have—*me*." Smiling, she squeezed his fingers.

"Marry me, Max," Michael said very quietly.

"I've got to go." Maxine stood up. "I told you it wasn't going to work out. I think we both like our comfort too much. Or something . . ." She felt a heaviness in her throat. Behind her long lashes, tears stood waiting. "Oh, hell!" she said and turned away.

"Max!" Michael called, stopping her. She turned to look at him. "What about tonight?"

"Eight o'clock," she said in a half-sob, "and bring some wine . . ." Fighting back the tears, she fled.

They came walking down Fifth Avenue, Harry Wald carrying the packages from Sulka under his arm. The fruit man was ebullient, happy with his many purchases and grateful that Sam had introduced him to the pleasure of spending money on fine things. "I love these silk ties," Wald said. "And it was a good idea, making those notes for me so I'll know which tie to wear with which suit."

"My pleasure," Sam said. "I think you went a little overboard with the underwear, though." After looking over Sulka's fine silk drawers, and letting them run through his fingers, Harry Wald had purchased a dozen pairs, one of which he had changed into at once. "How do they feel?"

"Fantastic," Wald said, smiling, "you ought to buy some."

"I'm a Fruit of the Loom man, myself."

"You should have let me buy *you* a couple of pairs, Sam. Why'd you stop me?"

Sam shrugged. "How can I accept silk underwear from a guy I don't know that well? God knows what you'll expect of me in return, and I'm not that kind of fella."

Wald was chuckling as they reached the parking garage where he had left his car that morning. "I appreciate what you've done for me, Sam. It's really fun to spend money. I never knew that."

"Especially when you've got it."

Harry handed in his parking ticket and the two men waited. Far off, a squeal of tires sounded. "So what can I do for you, Sam? Please, let me do something."

"Wear your new clothes in good health and look like a *mensh*," Sam said, "and make some woman happy.

Doris, if you're that lucky, or somebody else." A green Buick Electra came up the ramp at high speed and screeched to a stop. There was a dent in the fender, the left-rear hubcap was missing, and the car was nicked and scratched and badly needed a coat of wax. Sam was not surprised when Wald walked toward the car. Sam got into the passenger seat in front. Two pieces of tissue paper that had once wrapped persimmons were under his foot. "Home, James," Sam said. Wald buckled his seat belt, then pulled out into the street. "This is the car you took Doris out in?" Sam asked.

Wald nodded. "Almost three years old and sixty thousand miles on it. I give the car a lot of use, running here, running there." He glanced at Sam as they stopped for a traffic light. "Looks like hell, right?"

"Not terrific. Especially when you're trying to make an impression."

Wald looked thoughtful, nodded to himself. At the cross street of Fifty-seventh, instead of turning left toward Central Park, he turned right. "You got time for more shopping?"

"Sure," Sam said, "where are we heading?"

"There's a showroom over on First Avenue," Wald said. "Would you mind helping me shop for a car?"

Sixteen

"I don't want to talk about it, Sadie," Maxine was saying, "and I think it was very unfair of Michael to have called you."

"Why shouldn't he call me?" Sadie asked. "I'm a friend to both of you, I hope, so who else should he call—an enemy? And besides, I'm an official matchmaker these days, don't forget."

"I'm not on one of your cards," Maxine said.

"Of course not, you you I'm matchmaking for a Lucky Strike extra."

Maxine shifted the papers on her desk. She opened a file folder and took out a schedule. "Can we get down to work now? We do have three more programs to shoot."

"Shoot-shmoot," Sadie scoffed, "love and happiness is more important. I talked to Michael for about an hour. It sounds to me like you're both being very stubborn, and neither one of you wants to give an inch."

Maxine looked at Sadie and gave her a cool smile. "I don't want to talk about it, okay?"

"You and Michael, you both thought you could eat your bagel and have it too. But now you found out the truth—when you eat the bagel, only the hole is left."

"You're impossible!" Maxine exclaimed, losing her cool for once. "Look, I'm proving to myself that it just won't work with Michael and me because he's so stubborn."

Sadie shook her head. "You don't love him?" she asked quietly.

Maxine sighed. "That's not the point. I'm getting a kind of preview of what our life together would be, you see. We'd disagree all the time—he'd be inconsider—"

"He doesn't love you?" Sadie interrupted.

"Oh, God!" Maxine threw up her hands. "You have a one-track mind, Sadie. Nothing but love, love, love."

"You know something more important?" Sadie said, smiling. "You got a little disagreement going, my apartment or your apartment. Maxine, what's between a man and a woman is bigger than a lease, or a telephone number, or who is closer to the office and who'll have to take a taxi. I'm talking commitment, marriage, which is a contract signed by two people on earth, but witnessed by God, and believe me, *He* is bigger than any landlord.

"Marry the man, Maxine. You love him and he loves you. Trust in love, Maxine, and it'll work out."

Maxine did not reply at once, but busied herself with the papers on her desk. How easy it was for Sadie Shapiro to give advice, she thought. And how difficult it had been for herself to make the long journey through a man's world to this desk, this office, this responsible job. Marry Michael, indeed. The man would not bend, would not see things her way, no matter how great his love for her. She could picture him on some future day, using

144

that love against her, making her over, swaying her to his will, forcing sacrifices upon her. Well, she would not play the pliant maiden, not for Michael or any man. Let him give in and bend to her will, and if he would not it was better to know it now. "The subject is closed," Maxine said with finality. And it was.

The day was sunny but her feelings were dark. Sadie walked along Central Park South, on her way to see Doris Mandelbaum. She passed the great hotels that line the handsome wide avenue, seeing couples meeting, dashing in to lunch in dining rooms, to hold hands and glory in the sight of each other. She thanked God for sending her a Sam after so many dark years of widowhood, for sending her—surprisingly, astonishingly, unbelievably—another love.

What was happening to the young people today? So much freedom, so many avenues open, and yet they were walking away from love, which in her own mind always equaled marriage. Long ago she had recovered from the shock of seeing the way young people casually moved in with each other. Even among her own generation, people had done the same. But not for the same reasons. There was no try-out period for marriage then. It was sink or swim. Scary, yes, but you made a commitment and trusted it would work out. Sam had likened this living together business to a Broadway show opening in New Haven, "and if it plays out-of-town you bring it in to New York."

They called it a common-law marriage back in the old days, which at least used the word "marriage," and offered certain rights to the women involved. They didn't call it anything today. And they had no names for the people they lived with, although they had tried to find some. "My old man," was one she'd heard used by a young girl, so silly it made her laugh when she finally met the "old man," who was twenty-two.

Sadie crossed Madison Avenue and walked toward Park. Doris had promised lunch and time for a good long chat. And if I mention Harry Wald, she thought, surely she would be thrown out on her ear, even with Mrs. Mandelbaum's Park Avenue manners. In her handbag she carried the new card she had made for Harry. Harry Benjamin Wald, a new man being remade by Sam. But can a leopard change his spots, like a woman can change her mind? Who knows? She felt a surge of pity for poor Harry. What good is love if you love alone? And if you *live* alone? Doubly worse.

A doorman in a bright green uniform opened the door for her, then called upstairs on the intercom. Admitted through the inner door she crossed a splendid lobby and rose up in an elevator shiny with brass and polished wood. On the twelfth floor, she walked down a carpeted hallway, rounded a bend, and there was Doris Mandelbaum, looking out from an opened doorway.

"Sadie! Come in." She wore a pale tweed skirt and an ivory silk blouse. On her head, a fetching silk scarf tied back. On her face, a smile as bright as the sunshine outside.

"Look at you," Sadie exclaimed, taking her hand and squeezing it, "you've lost ten years somewhere since I last saw you. What happened?"

Smiling and pleased, Doris closed the door and showed Sadie into a wide and handsome living room that opened onto a terrace. "Nothing exciting, I'm afraid," Doris said. "The only thing new is my lipstick."

"From God's ears to your lips," Sadie joked, "it suits you." She looked around, drinking in the elegance of the

146

room. The floors were richly carpeted, the furniture polished and in good taste. A baby grand piano stood gleaming in a corner, topped with a group of photographs in silver frames. And there were more framed photos atop the mantelpiece of the fireplace on the near wall. "Beautiful!" Sadie said, a hand to her cheek in awe, "what a place." Built-in bookshelves ran floor to ceiling, the book jackets providing a focus of color and interest in the room. "You must be some reader," Sadie observed, "so many books!"

Doris shrugged. "What else do I have to do?"

"Can I see the rest of your place?"

"Come." Doris led her into a bedroom dominated by a wide bed with an antique Chinese-looking headboard. There was a small dressing room that connected with a bathroom large enough to hold a dance in. Coming back to the bedroom, Sadie stopped and looked at a framed photograph standing on Doris's dresser. A man's face, Jacob Mandelbaum it had to be, looking very young and smiling. A strong face, not handsome but close to it, with square chin and curly hair.

"My Jacob," Doris said quietly.

Sadie nodded. This face, this photograph on the dresser, this was what Doris saw each morning when she opened her eyes from sleep. As if being alone all night in that wide bed wasn't enough to remind her that he was gone.

"We'll have lunch on the terrace, if that's all right with you? It's such a lovely day."

"Fine and dandy," Sadie said with more enthusiasm than she felt.

The wide terrace gleamed in bright sunshine. In redwood windowboxes young marigolds were coming into bloom. Looking down the cross street, Sadie could see the pale shine of the East River.

"I made us a salad and I have fresh brioche," Doris said.

"Fresh what?"

"It's a kind of French roll." A glass-topped white metal table had been laid with linen napkins, china and silverware. "Sit down, Sadie, please. And relax. You look nervous."

"Who nervous, what nervous?" Sadie put a smile on her face and sat down. It wasn't nervousness she felt, exactly, but a kind of dread. Harry Wald was a dead duck, she knew, and it hurt. Where did that fruit man, even though rich, fit in here? A chicken can look at a farmer but it doesn't move into the house. Did she even again dare mention Harry's name to Doris?

Doris was busy portioning salad from a wide glass bowl. "It's a Niçoise," she said.

Sadie accepted her salad plate, opened her napkin. She waited until Doris had served herself then took up her fork. She poked through the salad, not recognizing most of the things in it, then tasted a small bite. "Oh," she said, "tuna salad. That I like."

"It has tuna in it," Doris agreed. "Try the brioche."

Sadie broke open the odd-shaped brown roll. She tasted it. "Not bad, a little like the *challa* my mother used to make." She swallowed a tiny piece of brioche, then put down her fork. Food was impossible now. She had come here to plead Harry Wald's case and, despite her feelings, she had better get on with it. Failure was also part of life, and it was failure she faced. "Got to talk to you about something," she began, "a someone who wants to get to know you better. A dear, sweet, lovely man I got to know better lately and who I like a lot. Doris, he's crazy about you."

"Do I know him?" Doris asked.

"Of course you know him, but not very well. Not well at all, Doris, and that's the thing about it . . ."

"Wait a minute." Doris put down her fork. "Not Harry Wald?"

"Yes, Harry Wald, of course, Harry Wald, and again Harry Wald."

"No."

"Why not, for heaven's sake?" Sadie protested, the words coming more easily now that she saw Doris was not picking up a knife to stab her in the chest. "You know somebody else in this world so in love with you?"

"The subject is closed!"

"The subject is love!" Sadie declared, "which is something you need and only one man I know is ready to give you right away. Harry Wald."

Doris's face was grim. "I saw Harry Wald twice, which was one more time than I needed to know all about him. He's not for me, period."

"What have you got against the man? Is he a Bloombeard or something, a murderer? Give the man another chance, Doris. You're liable to find out he's in love with you."

Doris shook her head, amazed that Sadie could go on and on when she presumed the subject had been closed. "Not interested," she said.

"Then who would interest you? That's what I can't figure out. How many men did Sarah Barish send you, Doris? Twelve?"

"Enough."

"And on your own, Doris, how many men have you met? Plenty, I'll bet. And so far, nothing, right?"

"You can see that, can't you?" Doris said in an angry way. "Look, Sadie, I like you and I trust you. But please don't get too personal with me."

"Hoo hah!" Sadie said, putting an edge in her own voice, "*personal.* What could be more personal, my dear Doris Mandelbaum, than going out and finding a husband for you? I'm a matchmaker, God help me, it's not like I'm a baker sending up a dozen fancy French rolls, which if they put more butter in you could die of cholesterol poisoning, you should excuse me. Someone to live with is the most personal thing there is."

"I won't see Harry Wald again. So don't waste your time."

"Better you should waste *your* time, right, looking for a man who died years ago to come back again?"

Doris blanched, her hands clutched the edge of the table. "How dare you?" she whispered.

"I dare, I dare," Sadie said, rising from the table to walk a few steps along the terrace, "because I know about being a widow, believe me I know. How your heart breaks every day, thinking about what you lost, how you think when it's six o'clock the door will open and he'll come walking in, how you wake in the night sometime and roll over in sleep and reach for him. . . . Only he's not there, Doris, no, not there and will never be there again. Not your Jacob and not, let him rest, my dear sweet Reuben."

Doris's chair scraped on the brick floor as she pulled herself back from the table. But Sadie put a hand on her shoulder and held her in place. "It's time to stop running away," she said. "Life goes on, even though you don't want it to, and widows are left to weep. I cried a long time for him, Doris, like you for yours, and I looked for him again in other men. But God is not as smart as we are. He hasn't invented a Xerox machine to send you a copy of your Jacob. But if you don't open up your mind and your heart to someone new, you'll live a long time alone. Like I did."

Doris sat in her chair, her head turned away. If she was crying it was somewhere deep inside, where even a woman as wise as Sadie Shapiro could not see. Sadie was silent, looking at the tiny buds on the marigolds that soon would open and flower.

"I was lucky," she said, "I found someone. As different from my Reuben as day from night. Reuben was small and quiet and soft-spoken and very sweet. And then I met my Sam, who was big, and funny, and made jokes and smoked smelly cigars which I hated, and wanted to move in with me and make moofki-poofki, without getting married or anything. But somehow, Doris, some way which we can never understand, that very different man became my love, my husband, the greatest thing in my life. I've asked myself so many times, how could it happen? And the only answer I can find is that when I was ready to let myself love him—God in Heaven—I found I did."

With a rush, a napkin pressed to her lips, Doris Mandelbaum ran from the terrace and into the apartment.

Sadie sighed, feeling sorry for Doris and also Harry Wald. She had tried and failed. But she had also said some things to Doris that needed saying. Tears were temporary, but Doris's pain was not. All right, Sadie said to herself, now you find out how a Park Avenue lady throws you out of her house. She was probably calling downstairs right this moment. Who would come to haul her away, the doorman, a porter? She'd find out soon.

Waiting, she sat down again. A hundred empty windows stared at her from across the street. She put her head back and closed her eyes, feeling the sun warm on her face.

Some time later she heard Doris stepping onto the terrace. Turning, she saw that the younger woman carried a tray. "I think we could both use a cup of tea," Doris said.

Sadie looked at her as she fussed with the tea things. If Doris had been crying, repairs had been made. It pleased Sadie to see that Doris's hands were steady as she poured through a silver tea strainer. She handed a cup of tea to Sadie. "Friends again?"

"Friends still," Sadie said. She put down the cup of tea.

"And no more Harry Wald. Promise?"

Sadie had to smile back at the younger woman. "Promise." She felt the need to move and rose, walking to the terrace railing. Goodbye, Harry Wald, she said to herself, I tried for you and failed. Her throat felt heavy, thinking of how she would have to say those awful words to the fruit man, and how badly he would feel. She looked down at the street below, watching the cars moving on the divided avenue. What do you do when you've tried and failed, and then you've tried and failed again? She thought of the new card in her purse with Harry Wald's name on it, and the fun they'd had writing the new card for the new Harry Benjamin Wald.

And the answer came to her.

"It's definitely time for you to meet a new man," she began, "and I got just the fella for you. His name is Ben Forest."

Over her teacup, Doris nodded, listening.

"Ben Forest," Sadie repeated, "he's in a lot of businesses and he owns land somewhere—out West, I think, something to do with agriculture. He's a little older than you and a widower. Does he sound interesting?"

"So far. What's he like?"

"Sweet as anything and very nice, besides. I think you'd click with him."

"Wealthy?" Doris asked.

"He's very rich, but doesn't like to admit it, which shows you how rich he really is. I know this much about him—he rides around in a brand-new car, shops only in the finest stores, and . . ." Sadie put a finger to her lips. "Don't repeat this but—he wears silk underwear."

Doris grinned. "My lips are sealed."

"Ben Forest," Sadie said again, repeating the name to make it more real for herself, "is a terrific man and the more I think about him the more I see him for you, Doris."

"Is he bright?"

"Very. Listen, the man is a college graduate and he reads a lot. *Two book clubs* he belongs to. I mean, is that what you call an intellectual or not?"

"Ben Forest," Doris said.

"Ben Forest."

"So far, so good," Doris said. "I'd like to meet him."

"Of course," Sadie said, "I'll arrange it as fast as I can." She came back to the table and sat down beside Doris. "You and Ben Forest, I can see it. But Doris, he's not at all like your Jacob. Can you accept that?"

Doris met Sadie's gaze. "Yes . . . I can."

"Good," Sadie beamed. "And when you meet him, you'll keep an open mind, promise me that."

"Promise."

"Wonderful," Sadie said. She put a spoonful of sugar in her tea. "You and Ben Forest—it sounds good." She stirred the tea, then took a sip. "Now all I got to do is talk *him* into meeting you."

Seventeen

"*Ben Forest?*" an incredulous Sam Beck was saying, "who the heck is Ben Forest?" He put his razor down and turned to look at Sadie, his face covered with lather.

"Ben Forest is Harry Wald," Sadie said easily. She ran a comb through her gray hair, twisting her head to check that it was lying flat in the back. "Forest, Wald—same thing. You know, a Rosen by any other name would still be Jewish." She turned her back on Sam and asked him to zip up her dress.

"It's crazy," Sam said. He dried his hands with a towel, then tugged up her zipper. "It'll never work, Sadie. Doris will be expecting to see some new guy at her door, and it's going to be Harry Wald, who she hates from the last picture."

"She doesn't hate him," Sadie corrected. "She just hasn't had time to see all his fine qualities yet. And besides, you yourself said that you've made a new man out of Harry." She turned and walked away into the bedroom.

154

Sam looked after her for a moment, then checked his face in the mirror. Same face, same shaving cream, he wasn't dreaming this. Hastily, he washed his face clean, picked up his cigar, and followed after his true love. "You've gone too far, Sadie," he said. "Harry Wald is still Harry Wald."

"Sometimes a leper can change his spots," Sadie said. She was transferring items from yesterday's handbag into today's. Keys, wallet, tissues, lipstick, Rolaids, Maalox ... "What did I do? A little wife lie, a piffle, a nothing. I stretched the truth a little, God forgive me. Was there any other way to give Harry another chance?"

Sam sat down in the bentwood rocking chair. "What chance? She's going to slam the door in his face the minute she sees him."

Sadie snapped today's handbag closed. "I'm not so sure," she said, "and besides, that's up to Doris. But I got a feeling she'll take pity on him, and the rest is up to Harry." She retied her belt, checked it in the mirror over the dresser, and started for the living room. "Luck," she said, "that's what Harry needs. A little luck, that can drop right into your lap something you couldn't reach even with a hundred stepladders."

Some years ago the Merchants Association of Fifth Avenue, working with a city agency, installed large concrete flower tubs at curbside from Fifty-ninth down to Forty-second Street. Trees were planted, to make Fifth Avenue green it was hoped, but over the years the trees have died. The tubs remain, however, a monument to the difficulty of sustaining life in New York City, at least among trees. Callous New Yorkers have made these soil filled tubs a repository for hot dog wrappers, soda cans, newspapers, discarded umbrellas, and other assorted trash.

Seated among the assorted trash, her jean-clad legs swinging idly, Brenda Fogelman saw Sadie Shapiro step out of a cab and come walking down the street. She called out to her.

Sadie stopped and looked, taking a moment to recognize Brenda. In another moment she was upset. "In garbage you sit? A young lady like you doesn't belong in there, out!" With a surprisingly strong hand, Sadie pulled Brenda to her feet. "And look at the way you're dressed! We talked on the phone, didn't we? Wear your best, I said."

Brenda looked down at herself. "This *is* my best."

A hand to her cheek, Sadie looked at Brenda in horror. "Paint on your jeans, army boots, and a man's shirt with a hole in one elbow? This is your best?"

For once, Brenda was abashed. "They were the cleanest, so I wore them."

Shooting pains went through Sadie's head and a stone shifted position in her chest. "We're going into a fine and beautiful place," she said, "and you're walking around like Tobacco Road. You don't own a dress?"

Brenda shook her head.

"I should have known," Sadie said, half to herself. "All right, they'll have to take you the way you are, come on."

But Brenda stood fast, her own temper beginning to flare. "Listen, I didn't *steal* these clothes. So don't lay any of that middle-class trash on me, okay?"

"What are you talking?" Sadie demanded, "and where could you even steal clothes like that?"

Brenda glowered. "I hate this hassling," she barked, "and I hate myself for agreeing to the idea of going in to be made beautiful." The way she said beautiful, it was almost a curse.

"Beautiful is what you are already," Sadie said. "What

they're going to do is make sure everyone can see it. So come on."

"All right," Brenda said, her lips set and grim, "but I'm warning you. The first biddy gives me lip or looks at me cross-eyed, I'll punch her out."

"You will not!" Sadie said, tightening her grip on Brenda into a squeeze. "You'll be nice and act like a lady, even if you don't know how. And the first rule is, keep your voice down, don't curse, and no punching anybody. Understand?"

Brenda glared at Sadie from under her overhanging eyebrows. "This is going to be one stupid day, so let's get it over with." With petulance flashing, she brushed past Sadie, almost knocking down a passing pedestrian, and opened the famous pink door.

Sadie followed her into the entrance foyer of the beauty salon. A young woman receptionist stood behind an elegant counter. The receptionist looked Brenda over. "Deliveries through the side entrance, please," she said.

Hastily, Sadie spoke up: "Mrs. Beck and Miss Fogelman. We're here for your famous Day of Beauty."

The receptionist looked from Brenda to Sadie, then back again. She consulted another staff member with an appointment schedule, found their names, and flutteringly apologized, then ushered them into a consulting room. It was a handsomely upholstered office, with red damask walls and matching carpet. Three of the walls were mirrored floor to ceiling, and a modish wire furniture grouping filled a corner. "Coffee or tea is available," the receptionist said. "One of our beauty counselors will be with you shortly to arrange your schedule.

Brenda and Sadie sat down, or rather Sadie sat and Brenda sprawled in the Molla chairs. Outside, down a short corridor, the receptionist sought out a young man wearing a white suit, white shirt and white tie, white shoes and flaming red socks. She brought him toward the consulting room, stopping a short distance away. The young man looked into the room and blanched. "Oh my Lord!"

The receptionist grinned. "Miss Fogelman and Mrs. Beck."

"The Amazon and her grandmother," the young man groaned. "Look at them, where does one start?"

"Think of it as a challenge." The receptionist marched off to her post.

The beauty counselor introduced himself as Mister Caswell. Searching for it among his trepidations, he found charm. "You will enjoy your day of beauty with us, we hope, being pampered and cosseted, and shown the essentials of a beautiful life in a beautiful body. No part of you will be overlooked, from hair style to hand care." He smiled benignly, trying to keep his eyes on Sadie and not Brenda. "I suggest we proceed from the bottom up. A pedicure first, then leg treatment, steam room, massage, mud pack, body oils, manicure, facial massage and moisturizing, upper arm and shoulder analysis, cellulite inspection and control, and then fanny shaping."

"My goodness," Sadie beamed, trying to get Brenda to show some interest, "that's a full day all right."

"That's only the morning," Caswell said. "After lunch we'll talk again." He led them to individual dressing rooms where they hung up their clothing and changed into shapeless, though comfortable, white cotton tent dresses.

In the pedicure room, a middle-aged foot specialist inspected Brenda's feet. "Poor dear," she clucked sadly, "you look as if you've been wearing army boots."

"I have," Brenda said through gritted teeth, but she

submitted to the treatment without complaint. Sadie, on the other foot, enjoyed it thoroughly.

In their next stop, the legs boutique, the woman who worked on legs could not believe Brenda's. "Haven't you ever shaved your legs?" she asked. Brenda growled a no.

"Twenty-five years' worth of hair you got there," Sadie said.

"I think shaving your legs is barbaric," Brenda said. "We're supposed to have hair on our legs, it's natural, it protects the skin."

"Brenda, we're not living in caves any more."

"Why can't we leave my leg hair alone?"

"Because, unfortunately, men leave women with hairy legs alone, too," Sadie said.

Brenda was not convinced. "European women don't shave their legs. They think leg hair is sexy."

"To a squirrel, yes," Sadie said, "maybe a pussycat. Fred Dubin is an American human being person."

Having said the magic name, Sadie stared down Brenda's withering look. The young girl grumbled on, but lay back and submitted to the treatment, although she did cover her eyes. Her legs were washed with warm water and then the operator dried them gently with a fluffy towel. Next, she began applying the wax. Brenda sat bolt upright, unbelieving. "My God, I'm being Simonized!" she wailed.

The day of beauty ticked on. Sadie and Brenda were steamed, mudpacked, bathed twice over in precious oils, then pounded and pummeled by a knowing Swedish masseuse until their bodies glowed with health. Every pore open to the world now, they napped briefly before moving on to the manicurist. This worthy, a kindly soul called only Schaeffer, was appalled by Brenda's hands. "Only once before have I seen hands as bad as yours," she said to Brenda, "on a lady from Tulsa who worked an oil rig." She plunged Brenda's hands into an emollient bath.

"I pound metal all day," Brenda said.

"I'm not surprised," Schaeffer nodded. "What kind of soap are you using on your hands?"

"Ajax Cleanser. It's the only thing that gets off the grime."

Schaeffer looked as if she were about to go into conniptions. "I'm surprised you have any skin left." She worked a full half hour on each of Brenda's hands, noting that her cuticles could only be fully restored through surgery.

Sometime later they lunched in a charming, small but airy room, picking at a variety of salads and drinking herbal tea. To Sadie's eyes, Brenda looked much improved already, and she said so. The steam and mud-packs had brought a glow to the young artist's face. "This isn't as bad as I thought it'd be," Brenda confessed. "I liked that steam room and the hard massage. It felt good."

"You would like that massage," Sadie grinned. "One more knock and I was about to slap that Swedish lady back."

Now there was only an afternoon of beauty left in the day. A wonderfully chic middle-aged woman, wearing a cotton shirtwaist starched to within an inch of its life, led them into her private beauty salon. "Call me Tamara," she said in a vaguely European accent. She sat Brenda in a barber chair and turned on a bank of lights that illuminated her face. Tamara studied her, not speaking, then walked around the chair to view her face from all angles. In a moment she picked up a sketchbook and began to draw. Three minutes later, a very good approximation of Brenda appeared on her pad. "Such a sensitive face," she said to Brenda, "you are artist?"

"Sculptor."

"Ah, yes, sensitive but with great strength too, yes?"

"Like a truck driver," Sadie agreed.

Tamara showed Brenda her sketch. "Cheekbones very good, eyes outstanding, chin is firm, very strong. These we do not touch, only to highlight them. Eyebrows now . . ." Tamara stared into Brenda's face, her own only a foot away.

"Now wait a minute," Brenda said, "you don't touch my eyebrows."

Tamara smiled. "I agree. They are your strongest feature. Perhaps only a little shaping, yes?" She took her pad and, using an eraser, redrew her sketch. She showed it to Brenda. "Only a small change, you see, but now eyebrows have a curve, a shape."

Brenda took her time studying the picture. Tamara was an artist in her own right, and with a few strokes had shown Brenda how to take a wild and bushy growth and change it to highlight her eyes and keynote her entire face. "I like it," Brenda said.

"Good," Tamara smiled. "Now for hair, I think we do this." She walked behind Brenda and seized the wild tangle of black hair that tumbled to the girl's shoulder blades. Pulling it back, she folded it in her hand and held it at shoulder length. In the mirror, Brenda could see the change. "Cut to this length, you see, and still you are *you*—not someone else."

"I don't want to be anyone else," Brenda said firmly.

Tamara nodded agreement. "Just so. You are unusual-looking girl. Wild and free, with gypsy dark eyes and hair. I think you do not often wash your hair, no?"

"When I think of it," Brenda shrugged.

Tamara smiled to herself. "Think of it once a week, at least, yes? And this haircut, you only have to brush for a few moments."

161

"I don't own a hairbrush," Brenda said.

"I give you one," Tamara said, "as a present from one artist to another." Perhaps it was the way she said this, or the good feeling Brenda felt at that moment, but something hopeful clicked inside Brenda and she nodded assent.

For the next thirty minutes Tamara washed and cut her hair, then dried it and brushed it out. "Little work, you see, and it stays," the beauty consultant said. She pushed a lever and Brenda was suddenly horizontal in the chair. Using a succession of instruments, some of them electrical, Tamara worked on Brenda's eyebrows until they looked exactly like the sketch. She levered Brenda upright in the chair so she could see herself in the mirror.

Standing behind her, Sadie gasped at the face in the mirror. It was Brenda all right, but a new Brenda, more sophisticated, confident, with bold dark eyes that leaped out and held her own.

"My God!" Brenda exclaimed. "I'm gorgeous!"

Tamara roared with laughter. "You are, yes. Now for finishing touches. Simple only." She took her makeup kit and seated herself before the young girl. With a brush, she applied a pale blusher to her cheeks. Then she gently covered her lips with a pale pink lipstick. The transformation was complete. The great strength of Brenda Fogelman, the wildness that was formerly only in her tangled hair and aggressive speech, was now in her face. Eyes that commanded attention, the molded high cheekbones that were always there but now were shown to advantage, that confident chin now wedded to generous lips that looked sweet and yet vulnerable, all of it held together by clear, ivory skin and a soft fall of shining black hair.

"Only these three things," Tamara said, "and you will

always be so beautiful. Wash and brush your hair, a touch of makeup on your cheeks, so, and always for you a pale lipstick. Lucky girl, to need so little."

Brenda nodded dumbly, awash in feeling so intense she could not speak. She squeezed Tamara's hand in thanks.

The rest of the day of beauty was an anticlimax. Brenda had become a different person, or so it seemed to Sadie. Because she was so beautiful, she walked differently, her voice sounded lower, quieter and less strident, her whole demeanor became softer, more womanly. From time to time, she looked at herself in the mirror, smiling very shyly, clearly very pleased. The first person to be captured by Brenda's stunning new look had been Brenda herself. The girl could walk out of here and appear on a fashion magazine cover, Sadie thought. She would never do that, of course, but never again would she appear in public looking like the wild woman of lower SoHo. Such beauty carried its own weight, and the impact on Brenda's life would be heavy. She was changing even now, before Sadie's eyes, accepting the responsibility of her own stunning appearance as a queen accepts her own station in life.

"Sadie, I never thought I could look like this," Brenda was saying as they left the beauty salon. "I still can't believe it."

"Believe it."

Brenda stopped to admire herself in a store window. "It's really me, though, isn't it? Me, Brenda Fogelman?"

"You're the same Brenda, only different. Like a Dr. Jekyll was hiding in you, a beautiful person inside a plain brown wrapper." Smiling, Sadie gave Brenda a playful pinch. "Fred Dubin," she announced, *"look out!"*

Eighteen

"Of course, I believe you," Sam was saying. "If you told me you taught Brenda Fogelman to fly I'd believe you." He opened his closet door and snapped on the interior light. Somewhere, in a plastic bag he hoped, he'd find his tuxedo. "Helping Harry Wald was nothing compared to changing Brenda. I hope Dubin notices."

Sadie was sitting on the edge of the bed, her fingers flying as she knitted quickly, using up a huge shopping bag of thin white wool. "Brenda's so beautiful now, if it won't be Dubin, it'll be somebody else, I'm sure of it. Men will fight over her like she's the last herring left in the barrel, that's how gorgeous she is."

"Let's hope she doesn't hit them on the head with her hammer." Sam pushed aside a couple of heavy tweed suits and found his tuxedo. "Here it is, the old soup and fish." He took it out of the closet and brought it close to the bedside lamp to inspect. It was clean and ready to wear. "Look at these old, wide lapels," he said, grinning, "so old they're back in style again. Would you believe I bought this tuxedo in Nineteen Thirty-nine?"

"Do you have a nice shirt, Sam? You'll be on television, you know; Fred Dubin said he'd show a lot of the crowd at the opening."

"I'll pick up a shirt this week. Probably at Sulka's, and maybe a couple of pairs of silk underwear. Harry Wald —excuse me—*Ben Forest* recommends them."

Sadie looked up from her crocheting. "Cross your fingers for Harry. Tonight's the night he's seeing Doris. I wish him good luck."

Sam rehung the tuxedo in his closet. "He'll need it. I expect a phone call any minute . . . Doris opened the door, took one look at Harry and slammed it in his face."

At that very moment there was a ring. Sam and Sadie both jumped, thinking for the moment it was the telephone, but it was the front doorbell.

Bryna Pernik and her grandmother were standing in the doorway, and Bryna carried a fruitcake on a tray. "Wait till you taste this," Bryna told Sam, "this is the real recipe, the genuine article, Sadie!" she called. "You have to try Maria Pernik's Special Hungarian Fruitcake, and I have to thank you for all you did."

Sadie emerged from the bedroom. She hugged Maria Pernik and kissed Bryna lightly on the cheek. "You don't have to thank me. Just seeing you two together is enough."

Ten minutes later they were seated around the kitchen table. Bryna made a small ceremony of cutting the cake, and passed the first piece to Sadie. It was, as Bryna said it would be, the best of fruitcakes, light, moist, and delicious.

"Wonderful," Sadie nodded, "and worth waiting for."

"I told you," Bryna beamed. "My grandma's recipe is the best."

"Let me confess something," Sam said. "I hate fruitcake, but I have to admit, if I was going to like fruitcake, I'd like this one."

Bryna looked at her grandmother. "I've made four of them since Grandma gave me her recipe. Each one better than the last." She reached out and took her grandmother's hand in her own. "I have a small confession to make, though. I made one, teeny-tiny change in the recipe, Grandma. You use only rum in the cake, and while it was terrific, I thought it would be better if I added two tablespoons of brandy. I think it makes the cake more moist."

Maria Pernik took another piece of fruitcake on her fork and tasted it. She looked at Bryna. "It is more moist. Good."

Bryna's dark eyes were serious. "You're not upset that I made a change in your recipe?"

"Upset?" Maria Pernik shook her head. "Better is better." Bryna looked relieved.

"Two tablespoons of brandy," Maria Pernik said. She winked at Sadie. "When I get home, I'll have to write that down."

The new silver gray Coupe de Ville paused for a light on Park Avenue. The odometer read 147 miles and the interior, lush and perfect, smelled faintly of rich wood and leather. Harry Wald's fingers drummed nervously on the steering wheel as he waited for the traffic light to change. In his pocket were two tickets to the Rubinstein piano recital at Lincoln Center. He had paid an outrageous amount for them, but they were worth it. Only the privileged few got to hear Rubinstein and tonight, he and Doris would be among them. They would, that is, if Doris went out with him at all.

The light broke, and Harry headed uptown. "When you've got it, flaunt it," Sam had said, "and more than that, enjoy it." Harry had to admit, he was enjoying it. This Cadillac, for example. For a decade now he had been able to afford a car this luxurious, but he had avoided owning one. Drive a Cadillac, some little inner voice always told him, and people will think you're rich. Never mind that you may, indeed, be rich, it isn't right to look it. Or act it. Why was that? And who started it?

No more of that, not for him. By heaven, spending money gives you a feeling of pleasure that you get no other way. Not to show off for other people, but for yourself. He'd worked hard enough to make it, that was for sure. So why had he denied himself all these years? Just silly, that's all.

He approached Doris's apartment building on Park Avenue and did not bother looking for a parking space. Instead, he pulled the powerful car to a smooth stop in front of the canopy that extended from the building to the street. The curb strip was painted yellow and a small sign announced: Positively No Parking. Harry switched off the ignition. He took two packages off the seat, a bouquet of a dozen pink camellias and a gold box of Godiva chocolates, then got out of the car. The doorman approached from the building, but before he could say anything Harry reached into his pocket, found a bill and handed it to the man. "I'll be a few minutes," Harry said. "Keep an eye on the car."

The doorman looked at the bill in his hand, saw Alexander Hamilton's portrait, and smiled. "Yes, sir. It'll be right there when you come down."

Harry checked himself in the vestibule mirror. Spotless blue blazer, gray slacks, Bally high-gloss loafers, and the bright striped tie Sam had selected to go with the baby blue chambray Paul Stuart shirt. Automatically, he centered his tie, smiling devilishly at himself. "Mrs. Mandelbaum, twelfth floor," he said, "tell her Ben Forest is here."

A moment later he was punching the elevator call button, staring into yet another mirror. Ben Forest, he told his image, you're a good-looking guy. He stepped into the elevator, feeling the soft cool swish of his silk shorts. He shot his cuffs, then ran his free hand down the sleeve of his blazer. It felt good. It was amazing what some new clothes, and a new attitude could do. Doris would be crazy not to go out with him because he was terrific. He stood tall, feeling thinner, elegant, and very sophisticated, as if he had inherited Fred Astaire's genes.

Humming to himself, he stepped off the elevator and walked down the carpeted hall. Ben Forest indeed. It was a trick, a funny trick, he thought, but at least he had one more chance at the woman he was crazy about. He paused in front of her door, suddenly nervous again. What if she turned him down—what then? The way you look, kid, he answered himself, not a chance. And if she does, came another thought, you'll find someone else. Comforted, albeit by himself, he pressed the doorbell.

Inside, he heard the clack of Doris's high heels as she came to the door. "Who is it?"

"Ben Forest," said Harry Wald.

Three antiburglar locks clicked, the door opened. Doris was standing there in a bright red wool dress. Doris Mandelbaum with a totally surprised look on her face.

"Hello, Doris."

She blinked twice, taking in his smile, the bright tie

knotted perfectly, the cut of his jacket, the way his hair was parted just so. "Where's Ben Forest?" she said.

He handed her the gold box of chocolates. "A token," he said.

She took the box and said nothing.

"Doris, I'm a new man . . . so I took a new name."

She shifted from one foot to the other, trying to make a decision. She felt hurt, disappointed, and yet part of her was intrigued. How could Harry have changed his appearance so much, and for the better? How could he get younger . . . taller . . . better-looking?

"Sadie thought you couldn't see the Forest for the Wald," he said. "Doris, take a chance, I won't let you down, I promise."

"Harry . . ." she said, still undecided. He did seem different, confident and assured, no longer hangdog Harry.

Harry handed her the bouquet of camellias. "You'd better put these in water," he said, "they're very fragile."

She took the flowers, cradling them against her breast, her other hand holding the chocolates. "Yes," she said. She took a backward step. "Well, I guess you'd better come in."

Much later they came back to the apartment laughing. "You're sure he's the same doorman? I could swear he wasn't," Harry was saying.

"The same. Michael Bradie is his name." Doris put her fur wrap on the hall table.

"He must think I'm Rockefeller," Harry grinned, "slipping him tens twice in one evening. It must be the Ben Forest in me."

Doris smiled. "What can I get you? Brandy? Coffee?" She smoothed her skirt over her hips.

169

"Coffee would be nice," Harry said.

They walked to the living room. "Sit down," she said, "I'll only be a few minutes." She turned and started for the kitchen. She measured out the water and coffee and put it on the stove, then slipped out of her shoes. Opening a cabinet, she found two place mats and put them on the table.

It had been a wonderful evening, full of surprises. Their seats at the recital had been down front and perfect. And the music was perfect, too. She'd listened to Rubinstein play Tchaikovsky, her heart soaring with the music, part of her wanting to cheer, part of her wanting to weep. Stealing glances at Harry, she saw that he had been moved as well.

She remembered the light grip on her arm as he guided her up the aisle after the performance, the quietly subdued ride to the restaurant for supper. How had Harry known that The Four Seasons was one of the special places she had always enjoyed with Jacob? Was it only chance? And his charming conversation at table, amusing, just right, and delivered with a look in his eyes of pure adoration. He was an interesting man, Harry Wald turned Ben Forest, a very interesting man indeed.

Doris was sitting on the couch, her legs tucked up beneath her skirt. Harry sat next to her. "Do you know, it's almost two o'clock in the morning?" he said. "Perhaps I'd better go."

"A few more minutes," she said. "You never finished telling me about the orange groves."

"That's right," Harry said, smiling. "I don't really like to talk about them too much."

"Why is that?"

Harry shrugged. "The way they came to me, perhaps,

through other people's misfortune. I never planted a tree in my life, you see, and maybe that's part of it, too.

"Anyway, I started with a fella down in Florida, one of my closest suppliers. There was a frost, he was over-extended and the bank called his loan. He called me, we'd known each other for years—I even visited him once with Emily when we were on vacation down there —and he asked for help. So I helped him." Harry stretched his arms, holding back a yawn. "Listen, I couldn't let him go out of business, lose his trees. So I became a half-owner of his groves. That's about it."

"How about your other places?"

"I got them the same way," Harry nodded. "Suppliers got into trouble and I helped out. You have to put your money somewhere, and I bought into suppliers when the chance came along. And I always insisted they keep running their places as my partners." Harry smiled. "Can you see me harvesting fruit? No way. But still, I've got some of the best men in the country farming for me— and themselves."

"In Florida, Arizona, Texas, and California, you said."

"And Hawaii. I forgot Hawaii," Harry chuckled. "Pine-apples."

To Harry's ears, Doris's laugh tinkled like crystal. "And I took you for a simple shnook," she said.

"I was, Doris, don't you see?" A frown creased his brow, then fled. "I never really woke up after Emily died. I was like a zombie, asleep, in a daze. Alive, but only walking around . . . just walking around . . ."

Something stirred in Doris as she looked at the pain on his face. She reached out and put a hand on his arm. "Yes, I know about that . . ."

"To lose someone so dear," he said in a husky voice, "so sweet, so loving . . . so young."

Doris sighed from deep within. "You never really get over it, do you?"

They sat in silence for a time, locked in the past. Harry's hand sought hers and held it.

"It's really late," he said quietly.

"Yes," she said. She gently squeezed his arm.

"But not too late," Harry said, turning to look at her. Their eyes met and held. She looked so perfect to him. Doris read his eyes and put a hand on his cheek. Slowly he moved to her and kissed her gently, chastely, on her cheek. She moved up against him, her head fitting perfectly under his chin, the scent of her hair a perfume that filled his heart. Tight he held her in the circle of his arms, rocking gently, until her own arms reached out to fill her need.

"Hold me," she whispered, "please Harry . . . just hold me awhile."

Nineteen

There are few things as satisfying as the beginning of a new love affair, even someone else's. Sam was walking around singing "Joy to the Wald," and Sadie looked like the cat that had eaten the canary, on toast. Harry Wald, bleary-eyed from lack of sleep, had dropped by the apartment to deliver a kiss, a hug, and an expensive bouquet of flowers to Sadie. For Sam, he had a dozen pairs of silk shorts. The man looked like a visitor from another planet, one where the inhabitants wore a perpetual smile. Happiness oozed from every pore as he spoke of the evening that had passed, and Doris's plans for the coming week.

"Just tell me when the wedding is going to be," Sadie kept saying.

"Soon, soon," Harry grinned, "you'll be the first to know."

"And remember Saturday night, you and Doris are invited to this party and sculpture showing."

"It's black tie, Harry," Sam said. "You got a tuxedo?"

Harry shook his head, and Sam led him to the door, planning yet another shopping trip. He came back smiling, walked over to Sadie and kissed her on the cheek. "That's for being such a good matchmaker."

"Don't give congratulations yet, Sam. They still got a way to go." She held up a bony hand, fingers conspicuously crossed.

"I don't count my chickens until they're matched. When the ring is on her finger, that's when I'll be sure. And speaking of fingers, keep them crossed for Brenda and Fred Dubin."

"I've thought about them," Sam said. He blew a smoke ring at the ceiling. "Sadie, he's not the marrying kind."

"Every man is the marrying kind, it just takes the right kind of girl."

"That's not Brenda."

Sadie's voice was a shrug. "How can you ever figure out who'll fall for who in this world? It's a mystery, Sam, to keep everybody on their toes and make life interesting. Who thought that Mrs. Kennedy would marry an old Greek man who wears glasses, even with all his money? Or my elegant friend Ida would marry a chicken-market man came home every night with feathers on his pants? We don't know who'll end up with who, I'm telling you. God sits up in heaven and makes matches down here on earth, and that's the way it is."

It was just possible that God sitting in heaven was looking for a little help that week. For as well as things were going for Harry and Doris—they spent each evening together that week and also Wednesday afternoon seeing a matinee on Broadway—that's how badly Michael and Maxine were getting along. They argued daily by telephone and passed a tense Tuesday night bickering over dinner at a local Italian restaurant. The strain be-

174

tween them was beginning to show on their faces. Maxine looked drawn and pale, Michael tense and nervous. Neither one would budge an inch. From Michael's point of view Maxine was making him jump through hoops to prove his love. It would be far easier for her to move in with him, he knew, and every argument of hers to the contrary could not dissuade him. For her part, Michael's stubborn insistence on having his own way was tangible proof to Maxine that their relationship could not progress beyond dating and friendship. Doctors thought themselves princes, she knew, but Michael was acting like a king, no, an emperor.

She would not discuss Michael with Sadie. They met twice that week, taping one show and a portion of another. Maxine made sure it was strictly business, too, no matter how many times Sadie attempted to draw her out. She knew what Sadie's message to her was, having heard it often enough. Give in, bend with the wind, the important thing is to be together, right? Wrong. Not now, not ever would she surrender her hard-won independence. Not even for a person as warm and loving, as perfect as Doctor Michael Newman.

Under Fred Dubin's direction a crew of five was working at Hymie Farrel's SoHo Gallery. Lighting men were stringing lights, a sound man was setting up a small recording studio at the rear of the display area, and Dubin was in the backroom office, worrying. "Where the hell is she?" he said for the tenth time.

"Artists," Hymie Farrel said, "they're all crazy. Especially Brenda. Don't fret, Dubin, she'll be here for the opening tomorrow. I haven't seen an artist yet would miss his own show, except one and he unfortunately died the night before."

Dubin sighed. "I wanted to have a run-through with

her. Maybe I can call her on the phone. What the hell was the name of that place where they call her? Bidey Baby Dolls? Baby Bidey Dolls?"

"I have her number someplace." The small rotund gallery owner rolled his Rolodex. "Bitsey Baby Dolls, here it is." He dialed the doll factory, and asked them to call the weirdo on the top floor. "Brenda? Hymie. Fred Dubin wants to talk to you." He handed the telephone to Dubin.

"Where the hell are you?" Dubin asked angrily.

"Working," Brenda said, "where else should I be?"

"Here, God dammit. I want to have a run-through with you, so you'll know what to do tomorrow night."

"I know what to do tomorrow night. Meanwhile I'm working and you're interrupting."

Dubin unleashed a string of expletives.

"Very nice, Dubin, is that the way you talk to a lady?"

"Lady!" Dubin exploded. "Since when?"

"You don't have to use those words, you know, you could say heck and darn."

Dubin took the receiver from his ear and looked at it, not sure he had heard Brenda correctly.

"Clean up your act, Dubin."

A light went on in Dubin's head, then began flashing on and off. "Sadie Shapiro! You've been talking to that woman, haven't you?"

"Why not? She's a friend of mine."

"Oh, God!" Dubin exclaimed. "Listen, I get enough of Sadie Shapiro on the exercise show. I don't want her interfering in this."

"She'll be at the opening tomorrow. I gave her four tickets."

Dubin groaned. "All right, I'll deal with that. But you . . . I want you here early tomorrow, understand? So I can show you where to stand and the kind of stuff I want on camera. Eight o'clock and not a minute later, get it?"

"I'll try."

"Try!" Dubin exploded. "Try! You get down here by eight or else!"

"Goodbye," Brenda said sweetly. Dubin heard a click at the other end of the line. Stupidly, unbelieving, he stared at the phone. Brenda Fogelman had hung up on him.

Doctor Michael Newman had hung up his white coat and was changing into his suit jacket when the intercom rang. He walked to his desk. "You have visitors, Doctor . . . Sadie Shapiro and a Mr. Beck."

Michael greeted them at his office door. "Sam, Sadie— what brings you to see me? I'm delighted."

"Don't be too sure," Sam said, rather mysteriously. "This wasn't my idea."

Michael escorted Sam and Sadie in and seated them before his desk. "Is anything wrong?" he asked.

Sadie's lips were compressed into a thin line. "Wrong, he says. What could be wrong? Only a man and a woman made for each other like bagels and lox, and acting like two idiots, that's all. It hurts my heart to look at you, knowing how Maxine loves you and you love her and meanwhile the two of you are a couple of icebergs in the ocean, drifting apart."

Michael sat down in his high-backed leather chair. "It's not exactly like that, Sadie."

"Close enough. I don't see things getting any warmer between you. Am I right?"

Michael considered a moment. "You're not wrong."

"So what's going to be with you two?"

Michael shrugged. "I don't know," he said. "We seem to have reached an impasse."

"If impasse means impossible, then I don't believe it. Anything in this world can be passed as long as there's love on both sides. You do love her, don't you?"

"I want to marry her, Sadie."

"This I know. And Maxine?"

"I'm sure she loves me too," Michael said.

Sadie looked at Michael, then at Sam, then at the heavens. "So what's the big problem?"

Slowly, Michael filled in the details for Sadie. About the decision to share each other's lives, and the argument over which of their apartments would be home. When he finished Sadie was staring at him, a look of astonishment on her face. "This is what the big fight was about? Your apartment or hers? If you'll excuse me, Michael, that's crazy, and it's also insane."

"It's not as simple as that, Sadie. For both of us this decision has become a matter of principle. If I let Maxine have her way now, at great inconvenience and trouble to myself, will I always have to accede to her in the future? And vice versa for Maxine. Will she be putting power in my hands by giving in now?" Michael spread his hands. "Not so simple, you see."

"Wrong! Very simple, but made very complicated by two people who want to have a stubborn contest." Sadie stood up and gathered her coat around herself. "Time to move," she said, "let's go, Michael."

"Go where?"

"To your apartment and then to Maxine's. It's time you let someone else in on this great problem of yours. So up from behind your desk, Doctor, and let's start rolling."

There are few things in life as powerful as an old woman with her mind made up. Especially when it was a Sadie Shapiro who would not take no for an answer. Michael found himself closing his office and walking around the corner with Sadie and Sam. Like an over-eager customs agent, she nosed about his apartment, inspecting closets for hanger room, peeking into his cupboards and wall oven, taking in the view from his living room window. "Nice," she pronounced at last, "really nice. Not the best place I've ever seen in my life—not with such a small foyer and only one closet you could hang a shoe rack on—but okay."

"I'm glad you like it," Michael grinned.

"And I'm sorry you do," Sadie shot back. "Wouldn't it be simple if you hated it here?"

"My office is around the corner," Michael began to explain all over again, "and the telephones—"

"Enough with the telephones," Sadie interrupted. "I think you love Ma Bell more than Maxine, believe me."

"It would really be very inconvenient to move, Sadie. Very."

"Oh, I'm sorry," Sadie said in an acid way, "I forgot. *In-con-ven-ient*." She made the word sound like an Islamic curse. "All right, I've seen enough. On to Maxine's place."

Michael looked at Sam, who rolled his eyes and shrugged. A short time later they were climbing the stairs in Maxine's brownstone. "A little more light they could use on the stairs," Sadie observed, "wouldn't hurt."

"Hello," Maxine said as she saw Michael in her doorway. And then she said hello again as Sadie and Sam walked past him. "What a nice surprise!"

"Don't be too sure," Sam said.

"But you should have told me you were coming. I haven't shopped or cleaned today."

"Not here to eat or inspect for dust," Sadie said. She stood in the middle of the living room and took it in. "The high ceilings are nice, but I'll bet it also gets cold in the winter."

"A little drafty," Maxine said. "What is this?"

Sadie couldn't answer because she had walked into the tiny kitchen. Maxine went after her, looking in from the doorway.

"This is the kitchen?" Sadie opened and closed the broom closet.

"They call it a kitchenette," Maxine said.

"I can see why. You put in all brand-new stuff and it wouldn't be a kitchen yet. There isn't enough room to swing a coat in here. How do you manage?"

"I eat out a lot," Maxine said.

Sadie walked right past Maxine, crossed the living room, bedroom bound. Maxine hurried to catch up. "God, I haven't made the bed. Sadie, don't go in there!"

Too late. Sadie was in no mood to consider the niceties of housekeeping. "I won't tell your mother," she said. She walked into the walk-in closet, came out shaking her head, then disappeared into the bathroom.

"Are you moving, Sadie?" Maxine called after her. "Are you looking for an apartment?"

Sadie came into view again, nodding sagely. "Looking *at*, not for. Looking at two people having some kind of apartment contest, like a poker game. I see your living room and I raise you one stall shower. I bid my telephones and call your fireplace. Two crazy kids, that's what I'm looking at, Maxine."

Now Maxine knew which way the wind was blowing and it brought the smell of trouble. "Wait a minute," she said, "I won't discuss my relationship with Michael."

"It's too late for that," Sam said from the doorway. "She's bigger than both of you."

Sadie shooed Maxine into the living room, made her sit down next to Michael on the couch. She went, protesting all the way, but she went. Sadie's look and hands were powerful, like some elemental force of nature. Maxine, sullen and grim, looked her in the eye. "Now you're going to browbeat me, right?"

"Wouldn't beat you with a brow or with a cow," Sadie said, "wouldn't lay even one finger on you, cookie."

"As long as I give up my independence," Maxine shot back.

"Ahah!" Sadie cried, one bony finger pointed aloft. "I knew we'd hear that word soon. Independence! Why does that always have to mean alone, Maxine? Can't independence be two people together for a change, each of them independent, yes, but also depending on each other? Listen, this country was made by people who wanted independence—and most of them were married!"

Maxine began to answer, then realized she didn't know the question.

"I'll give you another word, *spoiled*. Spoiled rotten, the two of you, my big-shot television producer and my important doctor. You can't be inconvenienced for a minute, God forbid you should have a hangnail you'll make a federal case out of it." She fixed her eyes on Michael. "You'd really rather have your telephones connected than be with Maxine?"

Michael shook his head. "That's not the point."

"Oh, excuse me," Sadie said mockingly. "You got a swell apartment over there on the East Side, Michael—five beautiful rooms and you can be lonely in every one of them. So what good is it if one day you go out and win the Noble Prize if there's nobody to tell about it when you come home?

"And you, Maxine—you want to live here or nowhere, right?"

"I like it here," Maxine said. "It's convenient and . . ."

"Again that word, convenient. Happiness is waiting and neither of you two will budge an inch. You fixed this place up very nice, Maxine, but there'll come a time when you'll want more warmth than that fireplace can give you. Talking about sharing and caring, and don't tell me about independence and being a woman alone. I was a woman alone once, when my Reuben passed away, and it's like half a loaf and half a life. A man doesn't have to be an enemy, he can be a help. Especially the right man, like your Michael."

"It's not just convenience, Sadie," Maxine said. "Our apartments have become a symbol, I think, a symbol of the problems Michael and I have in our relationship."

A strange light flared in Sadie's eyes and her voice increased in intensity. "I'll give you cymbals in a minute. I'd like to take your two heads and bang them together —*cymbals*! Maybe that's the only way to knock some sense into them."

With a withering look at Maxine and Michael, Sadie turned away and began to pace. For a long moment there was silence. Sadie seemed to collect her thoughts. Then she spoke. "What you two need is not a matchmaker. God knows you're made for each other, you belong together, and the children you'll have will be as smart and good-looking as the two of you. So if you don't need a matchmaker, what do you need? A *referee*. Someone to make a decision neither of you can make. Michael do you love this girl?"

"Like the air I breathe."

"Maxine, the truth now—do you love this man?"

The flush on her face answered for Maxine as she nodded.

"I now pronounce you man and apartment," Sam joked.

"Exactly," Sadie grinned. "A home is in your heart, not in four walls. I know people could live in a tent and be happy, as long as they're together. So listen to me good

182

—because I'll telling you what to do. Michael doesn't move in here, and Maxine, you don't move into Michael's place. What you do is you *both move*! Into someplace new that suits you both. Halfway between, as exact as possible, so both of you give up something. To get something even better."

"We both move?" Maxine said. Beside her on the couch, Michael was nodding. "She's not a Sadie, she's a Solomon," he said. "Maxine, I'm willing. I'll do anything to spend the rest of my life with you." There was a pleading, melting look on his face as he held Maxine's hands.

"I don't know," Maxine said.

"Let's talk about it," said Michael.

Sam crossed the room and took Sadie by the hand. "My dear, I think it's time we took a walk." Gently, he steered her toward the door. Looking back, as they closed the door behind them, Michael and Maxine were locked in each other's arms.

"How do you like that?" Sam said as they began walking home. "What they really needed was a real estate agent."

"And after that, a marriage license." For absolutely no reason at all, Sadie stood on tiptoe and kissed Sam's cheek.

"Behave yourself," he said, "I'm a married man."

Twenty

Hymie Farrel's SoHo Gallery was a double storefront on Lower Broadway, located between a restaurant and a butcher shop. Formerly an ironmongery, it had been transformed in the three years Farrel had owned the place into an arena of avant garde chic. The walls had been stripped down to the bare brick, an expensive teak tile floor had been laid throughout. The tin ceilings had long since been covered over with several coats of matte black paint and a grid system of theatrical lighting installed. But perhaps the most important fixture of the gallery was the Rolodex card file on Hymie's desk. Names were listed there, names, addresses and telephone numbers of New York's Beautiful People. Beautiful, to Hymie Farrel, meant money first of all, then some passing interest in art, and lastly a willingness to come and put oneself on display along with the art. They were all on Hymie's Rolodex; the Grenouille group, the disco crowd, the Wall Street and Park Avenue Real Money people, the media freaks (not too many of those), theater and movie stars who wanted to be where it was happening and carried their own crowd along with them. A few key names were also on Hymie's Rolodex, ten or fifteen people who actually opened their checkbooks from time to time and bought some art. They were among the first people invited to every opening.

His velvet dinner jacket shining under the lights, bow tie slightly askew but stylish, Hymie Farrel made a last minute inspection of the gallery. Two waiters manned the bar along one side wall, champagne glasses (plastic) filled with bubbly (New York State) at the ready, the three-piece band (Max Katz and his Katzenjammers) was in place and ready to go, the silent air-conditioning system was throwing cold air to counterbalance the heat of the lights and the mass of humanity who would pack the room, the sound man had tested his equipment, the cameraman had put down his 16mm Arriflex for the moment, the sculptures were all in place and gleaming, the large piece (now entitled American Woman) revolving on its platform, the printed brochures were stacked neatly on the front desk near the door with prices rather shyly listed on a separate sheet of mimeo paper, and Fred Dubin was out on the sidewalk going quietly crazy.

At a signal from Hymie the band began playing, the waiters toasted each other with champagne, and the doors were opened to admit the first guests. Hymie greeted them, put brochures in their hands, and headed out to the sidewalk to corral Fred Dubin. He was at the curb, one foot up on a fireplug, smoking a cigarette. "She's late," Dubin said.

"She's Brenda," Hymie shrugged. "Don't worry, she'll show up. Are your people all set?"

"Set." Dubin ground the cigarette butt under his heel.

He nervously straightened his velvet bow tie, looking over the long black limousine that had pulled to the curb. The rear door opened and a recognizable blond tennis pro emerged, followed by two stunning young women who might be starlets. The tennis player was wearing a cream dinner jacket that almost matched his hair. Hymie greeted the young man and his escorts and showed them to the door, then turned back to Dubin. "Wait inside, Freddie," he said, smiling, "I don't want you to frighten away the customers."

Dubin walked inside the gallery behind Hymie. "We'll start shooting some background stuff," he said, "the key shots we can't get until the idiot girl gets here—*if* she gets here."

"She's not a girl," Hymie said, "she's a woman, and like a woman she wants to make an entrance." He gently pushed Dubin toward the bar. "Drink some champagne —and if you want something stronger there's a bottle of Chivas in my office." Turning away, Hymie greeted an extremely tall ex-mayor of New York.

Half a mile north, Harry Wald turned his Cadillac onto Broadway. Like old married couples, Sam sat up front with Harry while Doris and Sadie shared the back seat. To Sadie's eyes, Sam and Harry looked splendid and elegant in their formal clothes, and the gleam in Harry's eyes whenever he looked at Doris gladdened her heart. Doris was giggly and bubbly as a teenager.

Two blocks away from the gallery they ran into a traffic jam, then found themselves in a long line of cars headed for the gallery. It was almost eight thirty by the time they decamped and fought their way through the crush to get inside. They smiled widely for Dubin's camera as they came through the doorway and Sadie found herself stepping on the director's toes. "Where is Brenda?" Sadie asked him, "I want to say hello."

"I wish I knew where the hell—heck—she was, I'd wring her neck," Dubin said.

"Don't wring and don't get excited," Sadie said. "She'll be here."

A phalanx of dinner-jacketed Texans swept by and Sadie was carried along with them to the center of the room. She looked about to locate Sam and found Michael Newman and Maxine instead. Michael handed her a glass of champagne and quarterbacked their move to an unoccupied space near the bar. "What a mob scene," Michael said, "fantastic. And some of them are even looking at the sculpture."

"They're really very good," Maxine said. "Strong stuff."

"If you knew the artist, you'd see why," Sadie grinned. "There isn't an ounce of fat on that girl, all muscle." She nudged Maxine with a finger. "So? Tell me things."

"About what?" Maxine said blandly.

"Cool like ice," Sadie said. "Come on, I'm dying to hear about you two. All day I walked around worrying. I would have called you seventeen times already, but Sam said leave you alone. Now tell me this instant what you decided because I'm jumping out of my skin."

"We didn't decide much," Maxine said with a shrug.

"Except that we love each other," said Michael.

"And we want to be together," Maxine said.

"Good . . . what else?"

"And we went looking at apartments today and we may have found one," he said.

"And one more thing," Maxine said, "we're getting married."

Suddenly, unaccountably, tears welled in Sadie's eyes and she felt her heart leap up. With what might have been a sob, she fell on Maxine and hugged her tight. Despite her sophistication, her years of toughening her hide to compete in a man's world, Maxine began crying too. While the band played a disco version of "April Showers" the two women clung to each other, crying with joy, until Michael's handkerchief began to pass between them.

A gray-bearded art critic for *The New York Times* passed by, accompanied by Fred Dubin, his cameraman and sound man. "No," the critic said, "I won't comment now except to say that, in the main, Miss Fogelman's use of texture and form is, unlike the present generation's thinking, very striking and original."

"Which means?" Dubin asked, holding the hand microphone under the critic's beard.

"She might be quite a find. You can read the rest of my comments in my review." The critic turned away and headed for the bar. Dubin turned away as well, his eyes sweeping the front of the room, looking for Brenda.

Suddenly, through a space in the crowd, through the bright lights and haze of tobacco smoke, he saw a vision enter the gallery, a finely made white mantilla framing dark hair, a white knitted dress, beautiful in its simplicity, clinging to a stunning figure, a face so lovely that it made him draw breath. Others noticed her, too, people were turning to look, and there was a buzz of voices as they speculated on who she might be. An instant later, he recognized her as Brenda Fogelman. He stood, rooted, not wanting to believe it but betrayed by the evidence before his eyes. A wave of anger rose in his throat.

"Brenda!" Sadie Shapiro shouted. With Sam's help she moved through the crowd to the young girl's side. Tears stood in Sadie's eyes as she took in her beauty.

"That dress," Sam said. "Sadie, it's the one you were knitting!"

"Better than I ever pictured," Sadie managed to say; "better than a thousand pictures." She reached out and touched Brenda's cheek gently.

"She's like a queen," Sam said, "like a fairy-tale princess. . . ."

"And I feel like one," Brenda said, smiling at Sadie.

"Brenda!" Fred Dubin shouted from across the room. He began angrily to shoulder his way through the crowd, sweeping aside a stockbroker and almost knocking down the star of a Broadway play. Ten feet away from Brenda he yelled at her, the centerpiece of the television show he had planned so carefully disappearing before his eyes. People stepped aside for this obvious maniac plunging through the crowd. "Upstart! Imbecile! What the hell are you playing at!" he shouted, oblivious to the stares of the people around them. He grasped her firmly by the arm and began pulling her to the door, shouldering the crowd aside.

Sam started forward to stop Fred Dubin, but found himself held by a small, though powerful, hand.

"No, Sam," Sadie said, "not now."

A cold seething rage filled Dubin as he half dragged, half pushed Brenda outside the gallery and onto the street. His carefully planned show was *kaput*, killed by an idiot girl who had opted for glamour behind his back. How dare she be so conventional, so middle class? She was Brenda Fogelman, an artist, a sculptress, an original with a rare talent for being herself. Squeezing her arm so tightly it must have hurt, he pulled her away from the gallery and down the street. Before the windows of the restaurant next door he turned her roughly to face him. "Who put you up to this?" be barked.

"Freddie . . ." she whispered through tight lips.

"Idiot!" he roared at her.

"I'm sorry . . ."

A neon sign, blinking on and off in the restaurant window, illuminated the catchlight in Brenda's eyes. "Oh, God," Dubin moaned, "you cut your hair." He fingered the tips of her hair as it lay just above her white shoulders. "And lipstick . . ." Only now did he see the rest of the transformation that had taken place. Those dark gypsy eyes, shining with tears, the hollows in her cheeks beneath finely wrought bones, the tender trembling mouth so vulnerable in pink. "You've ruined everything," he said. "Why?"

A single tear escaped Brenda's eyes and started down her cheek. A crying madonna, she whispered, "Freddie, please . . ."

"I ought to kill you," he said less roughly. One hand, acting at no command, wiped gently at her tear. "Brenda," he said, and then, as he started to say more, found he could not. For a thickness had invaded his throat, a wave of feeling so sharp he could not speak.

"I love you," Brenda said.

He nodded, not knowing why, his hands framed her face. "Yes," he said, "yes." His eyes were fixed and slightly glazed as he looked into the face of this woman who only yesterday had been a tomboy, and for the first time in his thirty-seven years a shaft of love shot through his chest and pierced his wildly beating heart.

"Brenda," he croaked, his voice a stranger to his ears, "Brenda," and he swept her roughly into his arms, the scent of her hair filling his senses, the feel of her body locked to his, the warmth of her hand caressing his cheek.

He kissed those pink lips, softly at first and then with ever increasing feeling, and for a long time they did not say anything more.

Twenty-One

The first cold wind of September rattled the window-panes as it swept across the open space of Central Park. Sadie Shapiro poured water into the glass kettle and put it on the stove to boil. Sam had been sleeping for half an hour, but Sadie had too much on her mind this night to settle down beside him. Pictures kept coming to her, pictures collected over a warm and sunshiny summer.

How lovely Doris had looked that day in the rabbi's study as she and Harry were married. And how elegant and charming was the groom, in a well-cut suit of blue bought specially for the ceremony. How wonderful to know that love can sometimes come twice.

And just this afternoon, she had seen Brenda and Fred off on their honeymoon. They were taking a tour of Italy, with brave plans to see every piece of sculpture from Milan to Rome. That is, if they could manage to stop looking at each other.

191

Not far away, Michael and Maxine were probably asleep in their new apartment. It had hurt her heart to see them move in with each other without benefit of marriage, but these were modern times. Soon, soon, Maxine would name the day and their marriage would take place. For the prince she had feared would rule her life had proved to be a willing slave, doting on her every wish, and filling her days with comfort and joy. Before the year was out she would dance at their wedding.

The water on the stove began to boil and brought Sadie back to the world. She turned off the burner, then went to the cabinet and took down a box of tea bags. She poured the water into a mug, then put a tea bag into it.

Her eye fell on the old tin tea box atop the refrigerator and she brought this to the table along with her mug of brewing tea. She opened the tin box and took out the three cards Sarah Barish had passed along to her as a last bequest. Harry Wald . . . Doris Mandelbaum . . . Brenda Fogelman.

She looked for a moment at the three cards, then put them into the pocket of her robe. The old tin box was empty now, the work of a lifetime completed.

Smiling, Sadie began to fill the old tin box with tea.